GOI

Going West

VIVIAN SINCLAIR

Copyright

This book is a work of fiction. Names, characters, and incidents either are the product of the author's imagination or are used fictitiously. Any resemblance to actual persons, living or dead, or events is entirely coincidental.

Cover design: Vivian Sinclair

Cover illustrations credit:
© Hlewk | Dreamstime

To find out about new releases and about other books written by Vivian Sinclair visit her website at VivianSinclairBooks.com or follow her on the Author page at Amazon, Facebook at Vivian Sinclair Books, or on GoodReads.com

Tales Of Old Wyoming – western historical fiction

Book 1 – The Younger Brother

Book 2 – A Stranger in Town

Book 3 – Going West

Book 4 – The Revenge

Old West Wyoming - western historical fiction

Book 1 - A Western Christmas

Book 2 - The Train To Laramie

Book 3 - The Last Stagecoach

White Christmas Dream – Christmas novels

Book 1 – A Candle In The Window

Book 2 – Christmas At The Ranch

Book 3 – Forgiveness At Christmas

Maitland Legacy, A Family Saga - western contemporary fiction

Book 1 – Lost In Wyoming – Lance's story

Book 2 – Moon Over Laramie – Tristan's story

Book 3 – Christmas In Cheyenne – Raul's story

Wyoming Christmas Trilogy – western contemporary fiction

Book 1 – Footprints In The Snow – Tom's story

Book 2 – A Visitor For Christmas – Brianna's story

Book 3 – Trapped On The Mountain – Chris' story

Summer Days In Wyoming Trilogy - western contemporary fiction

GOING WEST

Book 1 – A Ride In The Afternoon - the Sheriff's story

Book 2 – Fire At Midnight - the Deputy's story

Book 3 – Misty Meadows At Dawn - the Soldier's story

Return To Wyoming - western contemporary fiction

Book 1 - The Christmas Gift

Book 2 - Coming Home For Christmas

Book 3 - Blue Christmas

Book 4 – On A Frosty Christmas Night

Starting Over In Wyoming –western contemporary fiction

Book 1 – Riding Alone

Book 2 – The Old Homestead

Book 3 – On the Hunt

Seattle Rain - women's fiction novels

Book 1 - A Walk In The Rain

Book 2 – Rain, Again!

Book 3 – After The Rain

Virginia Lovers - contemporary romance

Book 1 – Alexandra's Garden

Book 2 – Ariel's Summer Vacation

Book 3 – Lulu's Christmas Wish

A Guest At The Ranch – western contemporary romance

Storm In A Glass Of Water – a small town story

CHAPTER 1

Wyoming Territory, fall of 1888

"Where are you going, Miss?" the younger cowboy turned to the quiet pretty lady, smartly dressed, who was sitting near the window, looking outside at the rapidly changing scenery. She kept aloof and didn't take part in the conversation the other travelers had waiting to pass the time until the train reached Laramie. Since they left Cheyenne, she pretended to be lost in thought and talked to no one.

This didn't discourage the young cowboy. Women were scarce in the west and after all, she was a young woman traveling alone. She was pleasing to the eye and had to be looking for a husband. What other business could she have here?

She considered not answering, then changed her mind. Looking down her nose at the young cowboy, she answered curtly, "Going west" in a tone that invited no other questions, and showed the desire of the woman not to be importuned further.

Crestfallen, the cowboy's face fell at such a distinct rebuff.

To spare him more embarrassment, John Gorman intervened, making a joke out of it. "Aren't we all going west? In fact, we are in the western territories," he said and looked at the haughty lady, daring her to answer him with the same disdain. She was the first who turned away, pretending once more to look outside at the barren prairie.

The conversation stalled and lulled by the rhythmic movement of the train on tracks, some of the travelers closed their eyes and fell asleep.

John took this opportunity to study the woman near the window. Once the tension passed, her ramrod straight posture relaxed. Her clothes were of very good quality and of the latest fashion, proving that she had an easy and wealthy life. Then why was she on the train going west, as she said, unaccompanied and, as such, exposed to undesirable advances? Was she running away from a severe father or an unwanted suitor?

She was pretty, he supposed, if a man liked temperamental brunettes, with eyes flashing when angered. Not him, though. John still kept in his heart the image of a blond and blue-eyed angel, lost to him forever. He'd been in love with the sweet Esmé, the sister of his neighbor Lloyd Richardson, from the first moment he'd seen her. It had been more than a year since the lovely Esmé had vanished. The family claimed she had moved to her aunt in Chicago, but people in town said that she had died of a broken heart when her outlaw lover was shot by a bounty hunter.

Whatever the truth, John was not one to give up. What people didn't know was that he'd asked Esmé to marry him and she'd told him straight that she loved another. John accepted her rejection, but he couldn't forget her, not even after she disappeared.

"Hmm, do you think there are robbers who could attack this train?" a middle aged matron, modestly dressed, sitting across the aisle from John, asked him. At first, he thought she accompanied the young lady with a temper, but they didn't exchange any words until now, and the older woman had eaten a lunch she'd brought with her. Now, shaking the crumbs on the floor, she worried about robbers.

"There were some attacks, but not lately," John answered truthfully. "The Union Pacific Railroad company took measures to step up security on the trains or people would be afraid to travel."

The young woman at the window turned her head to him ready to ask him something. Her eyes were blue and her complexion peachy cream. She was beautiful, John conceded. No wonder the cowboy wanted to know more about her. Then he remembered her disdainful answer and his liking tempered down.

Just then, with a mighty screech of the wheels, the train stopped on the tracks. Luggage fell, people cried and jostled one another from the sudden change in motion.

"We're being attacked by outlaws," the

matron shouted, covering her face with her hands, like this would protect her somehow not to be seen.

"Calm down, ma'am. Your panic is not helpful," John told her, exasperated. With surprise, he saw that the only one unfazed by this unexpected stop was the young elegant woman. She kept her mysterious half-smile, arranged her hat back in the position where it was before becoming dislodged and turned back to look outside at the now static prairie landscape.

The door of the carriage opened and the conductor came in. "Don't worry, folks. We stopped to take water for the locomotive. We made good time. We'll be in Laramie in half an hour."

True to his word, the train started moving again after five minutes, and they were in Laramie half an hour later.

John was impatient to be home. His cattle had sold at record price in Kansas City, and now he was assured for the winter to come. Contrary to his family's predictions that he'd never amount to much and his ranch would fail, he'd made it successful. Of course, a bad winter could wipe out a rancher's cattle, but he would do his best and work hard to avoid disaster. There was no alternative. He'd burned his bridges when he'd left the family business in Philadelphia.

He opened the door of the carriage and when the train stopped he jumped eagerly on the platform carrying his portmanteau in his hand. He looked for Renard, his newly hired foreman, who was supposed to wait for him with the wagon.

"Pardon me, sir," a hesitant voice called him.

He turned and saw the young elegant woman from the train. She was not haughty now. "Yes," he answered politely, but impatient to find his man and go home.

"Could you please…" She wavered on her feet and raised her hand to her head hoping to chase away the weakness she felt. He moved closer in case she needed help. "Could you please point me to a hotel?"

No sooner had she finished the phrase that she

fainted dead away and fell in a heap at John's feet. John picked her up. What could he do? She was light as a feather despite the voluminous skirts she wore and numerous petticoats.

Timmy, the clerk at the train station approached him, looked at the woman and scratched his head. "Let's set her down here on this bench, sir. Is she sick? Maybe she laced her stays too tight or she is having a fit of vapors as women have sometimes?"

John knew nothing about lacing stays or fits of vapors. His mother had ruled the family and the business with an iron hand and was not faint of heart. "She asked me about a hotel. I think I'll take her to Kuster Hotel."

Practical as usual, Timmy picked up her reticule, dropped on ground near her portmanteau. He opened it and showed it to John. "She has no money, Mr. Gorman. I don't think she can pay for a hotel room."

"Probably not," John admitted. "All right. I'll pay for her to stay a few days at Kuster."

"Very generous of you, sir. But this won't help much. She can't pay for her meals and I doubt the delicate hands in those lacy gloves have seen a day of honest work." Timmy was blunt, saying it as it was. "In fact, if I were a betting man – and I'm not, 'cause my mama would tan my hide if I were – I'd say she fainted because her last meal was a few days ago."

An image flashed through John's mind. The lady had turned her head with a covetous look at the matron's plain bread and cheese sandwich. Only for a moment, before her eyes had shuttered and she'd turned back to look through the window. "You might be right, Timmy."

"She is probably one of them rich girls who run away from home and an unwanted suitor, thinking the world would bend to do their bidding, only to discover that it's a hard life out there. I've seen many like her. Some ended well, some in Tom Wilkes saloon."

Another trouble added to John's pile. His foreman didn't come with a wagon as instructed, so

John had no transportation and now he felt responsible for this starving damsel in distress. "Have you seen, Renard, my foreman? He was supposed to wait for me here at the station with a wagon."

Timmy shook his head. "No sir. I haven't seen him at all. But if you're in need of a horse, I have a buggy that I rent to the travelers new to town. It has been so much in demand that I'm thinking of buying a second one."

John laughed. "You're very enterprising, Timmy. Good for you. How much is the rent."

Timmy beamed at the praise. "For you, nothing. You're one of us and you helped me countless times."

"Business is business. Let's carry the lady to the buggy."

The buggy was a colorful vehicle, painted blue with pink fringes. John imagined that his men would laugh themselves silly when they saw him arriving at the ranch in such a way and with the fainted lady near him. After that, he was going to fire them all for not coming at the train depot as he'd instructed in his telegram.

"Where did you get this, Timmy?" he asked. If it belonged to one of the girls at the saloon before selling it to Timmy, John was not going to parade through town driving it. A man had his dignity. He'd rather walk home than drive the buggy.

"I bought it from Pierce Monroe. It belonged to Miss Vanessa. She left town as you know. And good riddance, I'd say. You don't like the buggy? It had also tiny bells attached to the top, but the travelers didn't like it and I took them down."

Yes, it could have been worse, John thought. Not only pink fringes, but also bells to attract attention.

The lady started to moan as soon as they placed her on the seat. She blinked and opened her cornflower blue eyes. "Where am I?"

Timmy took off his cap and waved it with a courteous bow. "In Laramie, Wyoming Territory, miss. Where did you want to be?"

"In San Francisco, but I guess I'm not there," she whispered.

"No, ma'am. You bought your ticket only to Laramie, no farther," Timmy explained patiently. Then he searched his pockets and took out a large sandwich wrapped in plain brown paper. "Here, take a bite. It's good and fresh. My mama gave it to me this morning. It will cure the faintness that you feel."

"No, I couldn't," she protested feebly. But temptation and hunger were too great and she took a dainty bite.

"Thank you, Timmy," John said and shook hands with the young clerk. "I'll send one of my men back with the buggy." Then he vaulted up on the seat and drove away.

CHAPTER 2

At the first street corner, he almost ran over a man sitting on top of a huge wheel trying to move by pedaling frantically. The man was wobbly and turned abruptly in the path of John's buggy. With the same sharp movements, he then turned in opposite direction and vanished into an alley.

John stopped the buggy and wiped his brow. "Good Heavens! What was that?"

The woman chuckled amused. It seemed that finishing the sandwich she recovered her strength and her voice. "It is called a bicycle. They are quite popular in Philadelphia."

"A bicycle? I saw only one wheel."

"There was a second one much smaller in the back that assures the balance," she explained.

"Why a man would climb on that contraption and make a fool of himself, I don't know. Give me a good horse any day and I'm riding like the wind," John muttered and making a clicking sound he started the buggy again. Come to think of it, compared to the man on the wheel, his pink fringed buggy was not so ridiculous.

The houses were fewer and fewer and soon they were on the road out of town.

"Aren't you taking me to a hotel?" the woman asked looking around with anxiety.

John stopped the buggy and turned to her. "Look, I could take you to the hotel as I intended, but Timmy pointed out that you have no money."

"How do you know I don't?"

"He guessed and then looked in your reticule. We are practical souls here. Even if I pay your hotel room for a couple of days, how do you plan on earning a living? Do you know to cook, sew dresses, do laundry, or clean rooms? These are the decent occupations for women, unless you want to sing at the saloon."

She bit her lower lip as her anxiety increased. It seemed so simple to board the train to escape and to make her way to San Francisco to the safety of her

Aunt Clara. She gave the clerk at the rail station all her money and asked for a ticket west. The money was enough to buy a ticket only to Laramie in the Wyoming Territory. Now what was she to do?

"I figured that the best for you would be to have a safe place to sleep and food when you need, until you make up your mind what you want to do. That's why taking you with me to my ranch made sense. Otherwise, I have enough to deal with on my own, trust me," he explained. "It's up to you what you want to do." He was tired and annoyed. The days spent in Kansas City, ensuring the safety of his cattle until they were sold, then worrying about the money until it was safe in the bank and on its way to the bank in Laramie, all this took a toll. After the train travel on the uncomfortable wooden bench, he was ready for the food prepared by Cook and to sleep in his own bed. He was upset that no one showed up at the train depot to give him a ride home.

"I don't want to be a burden," she replied primly, torn between the need for shelter and the

uncertainty of going with this unknown man. He looked trustful, but one could never be sure. "Are you married?"

"No, and that might be a problem. The self-righteous people in town won't approve that you live in a bachelor's house."

She waved her hand unconcerned. "I could be your dear cousin from Philadelphia who came on a short visit on her way west." Strange, but she felt safer with this stranger she met on the train, than living alone at the hotel. And she had no money to pay for anything, even if he'd offered to cover the cost of the room. Her instinct told her that there was no danger to go with him. On the contrary. He had a protective, old kind of chivalry rarely seen in today's eastern men. "All right, I'll go with you," she announced regally.

John started the buggy without comment. He planned to let Cook, the only female in his male household, to take care of this unexpected guest. "What is your name?" he asked, not because he was

curious, but it seemed appropriate to know who was going to be a guest in his house.

"I'm Cecily Adrianne Richland-Stark. How do you do?"

"I could be better, what can I say."

"And your name is?" she asked raising her eyebrow and sitting ramrod straight in the seat.

"I'm John Gorman," he said looking at the darkening sky. He hoped to reach his ranch before dark. He'd wasted enough time with this lady. "We're not very formal around here. You may call me John."

"My parents called me Celia," she finally said in a small voice.

"Celia," he echoed. Definitely an improvement from the many names she came with.

He didn't finish saying her name when he sensed approaching riders even before seeing them. The small hair at his nape stood on end. He had a high sense of danger and it saved his life often by making him aware.

He stopped the buggy. There was no way to be

able to run away with the buggy faster than his attackers. There was a slim chance these were friends, but he doubted. From behind the seat he grabbed a blanket and gave it to the woman. "Riders coming. Place this over your head and dress, so they think you're a poor woman. And get down, in front of the seat."

"How do you know they are dangerous?"

"I can feel it. Now stay low." He checked his gun and the ammunition box in his portmanteau and cursed Renard for not waiting for him at the train station. He mostly regretted not having a rifle handy. With a rifle and without the woman to worry about, he could face off a whole gang of outlaws. Not to mention that his horse was able to outrun them anytime.

But this was the situation and he'd faced worse in his life and came on top.

The woman did what he asked and then from under her voluminous skirts she produced a Colt and expertly checked if it was properly charged. "Maybe

I'm not well prepared to what is asked of a woman in the west, but one thing I'm good at is aiming and shooting." Looking at his surprised face she nodded. "It's true. My parents insisted I know how to handle a gun when I announced I want to go west to see my Aunt Clara." She pointed to the side. "Here they come. Are they enemies?"

The answer became obvious when the three riders split trying to surround them. One of them even emitted a loud yowl of attack waving his rifle above his head.

"Let's see your aim, Celia. But don't forget to lay low," John said taking careful aim at the one coming toward him, waiting to get him close enough before pulling the trigger. A bullet grazed the side of the buggy, while another hit the dirt nearby.

A different sound, not a yowl, but a distress call let him know that Celia's bullet had found the target. His own shot made the rider to drop his rifle and grab his shoulder. John turned to look at Celia. The third rider stopped to help his wounded partner to mount up behind him in the saddle.

From a knoll at a distance, two other riders came galloping. The three attackers decided the odds were not in their favor and the easy prey they thought to find driving the buggy alone was armed and knew how to handle a gun. They turned around and rode away.

Celia pointed her gun to the two who were coming towards them.

John hastened to push her hand away. "These are friends."

"Are you sure?" she asked frowning, pumped by the encounter with danger. The hoity eastern lady had proven to be tough. Not a wilting violet this one.

"Yeah, I'm sure," he said watching the two men approaching.

Renard, his recently hired foreman, was a mountain of a man with red hair and beard. He was easily recognized even from a distance. French-Canadian by birth, he'd made his way south, first into the Dakotas, where the unruly town of Deadwood in the Black Hills suited him just fine. He was a wanderer at heart and moved on, south to the Laramie plateau, where last year he hired to work at Lloyd Richardson's ranch. He was hard-working and reliable, but one day he said Good-bye and left without explanation. After a few months he returned, and as John Gorman needed a foreman, he hired at Diamond G Ranch.

The man with him was younger and seemed familiar, although John was not sure if they'd met before.

"You sure gave them what they deserved, Boss," Renard said, rising in the saddle to look after the departing riders.

"Do you know them?" John asked loading his gun and placing it back in his holster.

"Yeah, they are three no-good squatters. Parker chased them away and now they thought you were easy picking, driving this buggy alone. They intended to scare you and rob you of whatever valuables you have, money, the woman."

The younger man smirked. “The pink fringes convinced them they had an easy prey for sure.”

John narrowed his eyes. He was very sensitive about the pink fringes and his image driving this buggy. “I don’t think I’ve met you before. Did you hire him, Renard?”

The giant redhead foreman nodded. “I did, Boss.”

“I hope he’s good with horses. We need a good wrangler.” What could he say? Something bugged him about this man, but he was not sure what and why. Besides he’d left his new foreman in charge in his absence so he had to trust his decisions. There was another issue more important to talk about. “Why didn’t you come to the train depot as I asked in the telegram? Didn’t you get it?”

Renard sobered at once. “I did, Boss, but I couldn’t. We had trouble. Big one, not like these clowns who tried to frighten and rob you. Toby didn’t come to work yesterday. I didn’t worry then. A man has a hangover or such and can’t come to work.

Although, Toby is not a drinker. When he didn't show up this morning either, I rode to his cabin to see what happened."

John had a bad feeling about this. Toby was a young man who showed up one day to ask for work. He had his sister and her little boy with him and they looked on the brink of despair and starvation. Toby was looking at him with pride and didn't ask for charity, only honest pay for work well done. John let them live in a remote cabin on his land and hired him for the spring round-up.

Toby proved to be a good worker and his shy and quiet sister came once a week to do laundry for all the ranch hands and to clean the house.

"So what happened?"

"I found them shot, all three of them. The sister and her little boy were dead. Toby had three gruesome wounds, in his leg, in his chest, and left shoulder. He bled a lot and the attackers left him for dead. I had to bury the sister and her son and say a prayer over their graves. I couldn't let them there,

prey to the buzzards. And I made a travois to carry Toby to the ranch. It took time and when I arrived back at the ranch it was too late to come to the train depot. I figured you'd go to Marty's Stable and get a horse."

Yes, in light of what happened to Toby, his foreman had more important things to do than coming to pick John up from the train. "How is Toby?"

"Still unconscious. I called Four Fingers from the Maitland Ranch. He patched Toby up the best he could. There was no time to come to town for the doctor. Toby is young and strong. Four Fingers has hopes he'll recover."

John hoped so too. He really liked the young man and it was such a shame what had happened to him and his sister. "But why was Toby attacked? They were so poor they took turns to eat having only one spoon and one plate between the three of them. There was nothing there to rob."

"I think robbery was not the intent. Toby

didn't talk much and didn't tell us much. This is the west and his story is his own. We didn't ask. But I think they were runaways and someone wanted revenge for whatever reason. Maybe Toby will tell us more when he recovers. I'm leaving tomorrow morning to go after the killers."

Renard was after all his own man. He was not asking permission from his boss to go. He was just informing John of his decision. Toby and his sister with the little boy deserved justice. Besides, if the killers were holed up in the mountains north of there, there was danger for all the ranchers living isolate in the area.

John's cattle were sold. Preparations for the upcoming winter could wait a few days. "I'll come with you."

CHAPTER 3

The night was fully upon them when they reached the ranch house. John stopped the buggy in front of the porch, jumped down and went to help Celia down. She'd kept the blanket wrapped around her to keep her warm.

The ranch hands walked out from wherever they were, to welcome their boss home. They were all subdued in light of the brutal attack on Toby, who was well liked by all. They didn't comment on the vehicle and its ornaments, but Celia's presence was a surprise.

"Lookee here, Boss got himself a woman," one of them remarked loudly.

John looked at him severely. "Watch your language boys in front of a lady," he reprimanded the cheeky cowboy. "This is…"

That's all the warning he could to give them before Celia dropped the blanket from her head and smiled. "…Cousin Celia from Philadelphia came west to see John, before traveling to San Francisco to visit our dear Aunt Clara."

Revealing that she was a true lady, bred in the East, brought a moment of silent surprise in the yard, until someone observed, "I didn't know you had a cousin in Philadelphia, Boss, not to mention a dear aunt in Frisco."

John nodded curtly. "Now you do. I'll see you all tomorrow."

The men dispersed slowly to the barn and the bunkhouse commenting on the day's events. Only Renard remained and the newly hired fellow. His superior smirk annoyed John and for some reason it made him uneasy. "What did you say your name was?"

"I didn't," was the insolent answer.

Perhaps John was too tired to have patience with verbal duel, but he'd had enough for this day. "If you choose to work here, you'll do what Renard tells you. No one will pry into your business as long as you do your work. I hope you're a good wrangler and know your way around horses."

Renard came forward. "Hmm, about that, Boss, he's not a wrangler."

Guiding Celia up the stairs to the porch, John stopped. "He's not a wrangler? Then why did you hire him?"

"Because we need him. His name is Wayne Dunbar and he's good with a gun," Renard replied in his direct way, not at all embarrassed to have disobeyed his boss's orders to hire a wrangler. "Look, we had cattle vanishing, squatters near Parker's ranch who intended to rob you, signs of an unwanted presence on the range and now this murder of Toby's family. I don't know if they are all connected, but I'd feel better with a guard around the place. I wanted to leave Wayne in charge until I come back."

"No way. I'm not going to leave a stranger in charge of my ranch. Mathias will take care of things in our absence. That is if I can't convince you to stay and let me chase after Toby's attackers."

As John predicted Renard refused. It was not

his habit to let others do his business. And he'd taken Toby's attack personally.

"Fair enough. We go together and Mathias will take care of the ranch in our absence," John concluded.

"Hired or not, I'll tag along," Wayne said, twirling a nasty looking Bowie knife.

The gesture triggered some forgotten memory and John turned to face him. "Wayne Dunbar, haven't you been on the attacked stagecoach from Walden this summer?"

"Yep, I was."

"You stayed in town for a while and then challenged Deputy McCarthy to a gunfight."

Wayne made a face of disgust. "He wouldn't face me, the coward."

John shook his head. "McCarthy is no coward. Be careful what you say about him. He is well liked in this town and people might take exception to such words. Without being a vain man to say so, I'm one of the best and fast gunmen out there. Very few are better than me. But I wouldn't try my luck against McCarthy. He's that good. The best that I've ever seen. He made you a favor by refusing to face you and in the end, to kill you."

After a moment of pause, Wayne inclined his head. "I respect your opinion, Mr. Gorman," he answered noncommittally.

John was not done yet. The idea to have the gunslinger hired on his ranch was unsettling, no matter what plans Renard had when he hired him. "If your only purpose for coming back to Laramie is to catch McCarthy unaware and provoke a gunfight, I warn you I won't stand for it. I don't know you, but I know and respect him. If Bill Monroe ever decides to retire, McCarthy is going to be elected sheriff. He does most of the work anyhow."

"No, that's not my purpose."

John weighed these words before answering. "Because Renard trusts you, you can stay. But I'll be watching you." Saying this, he pushed the door open and ushered Celia inside. She'd been unusually quiet and had listened to the conversation with interest, without protesting that she was cold or tired, and she probably was.

After the door closed behind them, she looked at him and said, “You were wrong.”

Not used to be contradicted - after all he was the boss here - John stopped in the kitchen doorway. “Why was I wrong?” This eastern lady presumed to know better his business and to criticize his decisions and it was very annoying.

“You didn’t ask him why he challenged the deputy to a gunfight. Maybe he had his own reasons. You just didn’t like him.”

“I didn’t like his attitude. I’ve met a lot of cocky fools like him who cause a senseless fight just to prove they are a faster draw.”

Their argument was interrupted by a short round woman with the hair braided and obvious Indian blood. She came out of the kitchen, wiping her hands in her apron. “Mister John, thank the good Lord you came back safe. Go wash your hands and come to eat. I made you roast beef with potatoes and your favorite huckleberry pie." She eyed Celia with interest, measuring her up and down, not embarrassed to be staring. "So, you followed my advice and got yourself hitched in Kansas City. Very good. She's a bit skinny under all the skirts she's wearing, but nothing that my good food can't put to rights."

"She's not…" John started to say.

"I'm Cousin Celia from Philadelphia, Mrs. Cook," Celia announced primly.

"Just Cook, dear. Cousin Celia, you say? Not his wife? Oh, people won't like this one bit. I'm not sure it's proper for you to stay in a bachelor's house."

"Nonsense. I'm his cousin and I came to visit him," Celia replied.

Eager to change the subject, John interfered. "How is Toby?"

"Poor mite was shot three times and bled a lot until that Red Fox brought him here. Four Fingers patched him up and now he's sleeping. And his sister and her child, both shot dead. What kind of men could do that to three innocent souls like them?"

John patted her arm. "Whoever they are we'll catch them and they'll face justice for what they've done. Renard and I will go after them tomorrow."

Nobody knew where Cook came from. One day she knocked on John's door and announced that she heard he needed a cook and here she was. They could call her Cook and no other name was given, no other details who she was and where she came from. In the two years since, John had come to value not only the good meals she prepared, but also her plain speaking and good sense. He was not ashamed to ask Cook's advice.

"Tell me, Cook, what do you think about the new man Renard hired in my absence?"

Cook smiled. "You find him brash and you two have already clashed. He is a cocky young man. My sense tells me he's good at the core, but only time will tell if I'm right."

"I'll keep an eye on him," John muttered.

"Please tell Celia where she is to sleep and give her some food. I have to see Toby first."

A gas lamp on the table was lighting the small room upstairs where Toby was lying in bed, unmoving with his eyes closed. The slight movement of his chest was the only sign that he was alive. Four Fingers was sitting in a rocking chair nearby looking at his patient.

"How is he?" John asked him in a low voice.

"He was badly wounded when Red Fox brought him in." For reasons known only to him, the old Indian refused to use Renard's French name, which annoyed the latter to no end. Otherwise, there was no quarrel between the two or John wouldn't have hired Renard. "I took out the bullets and cleaned his wounds. The poultice will help them heal. I don't think they'll turn putrid. He'll survive."

Four Fingers was not one to make such comment if he were not convinced it would be so. John breathed easier. Toby would survive.

"Did he say anything? Who attacked them?"

"No, nothing. Although, I believe he woke up when I took out the bullets and the pain was too great to bear."

John went closer to the bed. "Toby," he whispered.

The young man's eyelids fluttered open and his eyes were clouded with pain. "Becky?" he asked.

John touched his hand that was lying limp on the cover. "I'm afraid neither her, nor her little boy made it. Renard buried them there and said a prayer over their grave. Do you know who did this?"

Toby nodded imperceptibly. "Yeah. He found us at last and sent his men to get his revenge," he spoke haltingly.

"We'll go tomorrow after the killers. We'll bring them to justice," John tried to reassure him.

A loud sigh like a wail escaped the wounded man's chest. "You never will. No one can touch him even if you catch his hired killers." He turned his face to the wall and closed his eyes.

Whatever else John tried to find out, Toby was

done talking. Either because he was convinced it was useless, or because he'd lost hope entirely and was in the deep pit of despair where a human was overwhelmed by misery and sorrow.

CHAPTER 4

Next day didn't bring any more news about who'd ordered the senseless attack on Toby and his family. In truth, Toby didn't know who was the man his sister had run away from. Becky refused to name him and she got this frightened face whenever Toby tried to talk to her about him. Now she carried her secret into the grave with her. All Toby knew was that he was a very powerful man who'd abused her until she ran away with Toby's help and found shelter at John's ranch.

After that, Becky didn't want to talk about what happened to her, although she loved her sweet little boy.

"Dang, we know nothing useful, Renard," John said, saddling his horse and looking askance at Wayne Dunbar who was ready to go and talking to Celia.

The day was nice and warm, and Celia had come out on the porch. Wayne was looking at her with undisguised admiration and was making her laugh with some silly story about chasing a bull on the range.

Some men had the uncanny ability to flirt with women without being too obvious or making a pest of themselves. John had never been one of them. While he was considered handsome and quite a catch as the owner of a large, prosperous ranch, his attempts to court women had been abysmal, not that he'd attempted this many times. When it had mattered because he'd fallen in love, he had been rejected categorically. Since then, he'd given up on making a fool of himself. If that meant he was going to die a bachelor, then so be it. He'd rather never get married than go through another humiliating rejection.

He mounted his horse and without waiting for the others, he rode away giving free rein to his horse to run across the land.

When they reached the cabin that Toby and his sister had called home for the past two years, there was an eerie silence over the place.

John looked at the two fresh mounds with two makeshift crosses on top. He shook his head. "Poor Becky. Such a short life and so full of only hard work and pain."

"That's what it is for all of us," Renard commented from behind him. "There are also happy moments that make it worth living. Mathias' son used to bring her wildflowers every week when she came to the ranch house to do the laundry. She loved them. She clutched them to her chest and had tears in her eyes. She said that no one ever had given her any gift just because. She was a nice girl. I'll see her killers punished whatever it takes."

Renard was not a man of many words and this speech showed how deeply affected he'd been by these senseless killings.

John forced himself to push the strong emotions away and to study the place with neutral eyes and unaffected by grief. He had to find any possible clues about the attackers. It didn't rain overnight and their tracks were easy to follow, but he wanted much more, a reason why it had happened, a clue about the identity of the man who ordered it, a tangible lead to him.

Renard kneeled in the dirt studying the horse tracks. “They were three, coming from northeast. This horseshoe has a slightly bent shape and a nail protruding. We’re in luck. They are easy to follow. They left the same way they came. They’re probably holed up in the mountains somewhere.”

Wayne Dunbar who had circled the place pointed to a rock formation to the right. “Four. There were four. One waited near the rocks. Something spooked him and he dropped this small pistol. Not exactly a Derringer, but a gun more suitable to women or professional card players.”

John looked at it. Dunbar was right he had to admit. “Definitely not a gun worn by a cowboy or a gunfighter.”

“A coward’s gun,” Renard commented with disdain. “No western man worth his salt would carry a gun like this, to shoot like a coward when his opponent doesn't expect."

Inside the house, nothing was disturbed, a sign that the killers surprised their victims outside and they shot them to death. They didn't bother to go inside as their purpose was not to rob them.

Everything was spotless clean and on the stove a pot with a half-done stew was waiting to be finished. The stove was cold and the meal congealed now. Toby and his sisters were indeed very poor. There was nothing personal here, not a picture or even a toy. John regretted he'd never thought to send a toy to Becky's little boy to play with. Now it was too late and regrets were pointless, a wise man had told him.

A well read and worn Bible on the table was the only object that Toby might like to have and John pocketed it to give it to him.

There was nothing else of importance. Disappointed, John walked out of the cabin. Toby was welcome to continue to use it, but John doubted he'd want to come back here, to this place connected to the death of his dear ones.

Outside, the traces in the dirt and dried blood told the story of three victims surprised by a brutal attack.

Renard, who discovered the bodies told them what he thought it happened. "They shot the little boy first, I think, and Becky covered him with her body to protect him, but he was already dead. Then she was shot too. Toby fought one of the attackers and pulled him off his horse. You see, here," he said, pointing to a place where the dirt was disturbed by the fight.

Wayne Dunbar looked closer and moved his boot over the place. He hunkered down and with his gloved hand picked up a glittering object. "And what do we have here?"

Curious, John took it from his hand. It was a silver coin on a thick chain. The chain was broken. John turned the coin on the other side. "It's a Mexican coin from 1871." It was silver and on one side it said Republica Mexicana and had an eagle on it. On the other side, the marked value was 'un peso', the sun and a sword with a balance on it. Libertad and Ley - Liberty and Law.

"I dropped it there," Renard said. "Probably it belonged to Becky. She had it clutched in her hand. The only thing of value she had. She wanted to pay the attackers to spare their lives."

John shook his head. "I've never seen her wearing it. I don't think it was hers. I think she fought her attacker too and grabbed it from his throat."

Renard was not buying it. "Becky was not a fighter. She was a shy person, easily frightened."

"A mother can become a lioness when her cub is threatened." Gently, Wayne took the coin and the chain and dangled it again in front of his eyes. "I've seen this before in Tom Wilkes saloon at a card table. Someone was dangling it like that. Unfortunately, I don't remember who it was."

"You were too busy relieving hard-working cowboys of their earnings," John remarked with contempt. He was not a gambling man. As a rule, he was not going close to a poker table and he was not drinking spirits. In fact, he rarely went to the saloon. He was not abstinent, but he just preferred to keep his wits and his money to himself and to be always in control of the situation.

If he expected Wayne to protest or be offended, he was mistaken. Wayne continued to look at the silver coin, like hoping to trigger a more clear memory. "I was engaged in a game where money was not the main object. After searching a long time for a killer, I found him and I had every intention to make him pay."

"What happened?"

"He asked why, and I told him. He confirmed he killed the girl and had no regret. After that, he drew on me.... Or tried to do it. Next moment, he was dead." He gave the chain back to John. "So, you see, at the time, all my attention was on that man. There were four men at a table nearby. One of them had this chain in his hand and was dangling it like this." He frowned. "I'll remember more and I'll tell you. Now, let's go after the killers."

John pocketed the silver coin and the Bible in his saddle and they mounted their horses and rode toward northeast.

Renard was riding in front as he was the best tracker of the three. From time to time, he stopped to find new tracks or to retrace on a different path.

"Do you think it might be the three who attacked me when I returned from the train station?" John asked.

"No, those were just robbers. I know they would not hesitate to kill if they were paid to commit a crime, but in the world of lawless people, there are thieves and there are killers…" He stopped talking and made a sign for them to halt right there. He looked around and sniffed the air like the fox he was named after. "Smoke nearby."

"I hope not. It's been a dry season and fire made without care could light up in flames the whole prairie," John remarked unhappy.

Wayne dismounted. "I'll go and see." He climbed the hill and when he reached the top, he lay

down to look over on the other side. Satisfied, he waved his hat to signal that it was all clear, they could come over.

It was an abandoned camp. Recently abandoned. The fire was dying down, probably extinguished in haste as the campers were leaving. Some embers were still glowing.

"Do you think these are the men we are following, Renard?" John asked.

"No. The tracks run straight north. These are different men. Probably outlaws like the killers. The farther north we go, the wilder the area becomes, and there are fewer ranches as we get farther away from the railroad. Look, they butchered a calf and left it to rot. What a waste! They make me sick." Renard, born to a family of Canadian trappers had strict rules about slaughtering an animal. "Let's move on from here."

"Rustlers?" Wayne wondered.

"They stole the animal from one of the ranches, that's for sure. But as Renard said, there are

outlaws holed up in the wilderness north of here. Last year, the railroad from Cheyenne to Deadwood in the Dakotas was completed and as the civilization came in, the outlaws hid into the mountains and more remote areas."

There was nothing of interest abandoned in the camp, except a tin plate bent out of shape and a rusted can used for target.

The darkness was approaching swiftly. After riding all day, it was time to find a place to settle for the night. It was chilly to sleep outdoors, but they were used to it and they had extra blankets to keep them warm.

CHAPTER 5

They stopped for the night and made a small campfire in an open space chosen by Renard. "Near the rocks would be more protected from the cold, but easy to be attacked from above and we could be surrounded without a way out," he explained. "Like this, we can see any man coming our way."

It was good reasoning, John supposed, although he was uneasy to sleep exposed to all, with the fire so visible. He shrugged. He trusted Renard and at least it was not going to be a frosty night.

They were eating some cold beef, with bread and beans from a can heated over the fire. Beans were the usual food for cowboys working on the range. The fire was warming them, as did the hot coffee expertly prepared by Renard.

The rugged foreman raised his eyes and scrutinized the darkness around them. He set his cup on the ground near him and grabbed his rifle. "We have a visitor."

Soon, John saw him too, and he checked his gun and placed his own rifle handy.

In his own quiet way, Wayne rose and without a word vanished into the night.

"He's going to check if there are others hidden around waiting to attack us," Renard explained.

For a brief moment, John envied the easy way his foreman and the newly hired man understood each other, like two true western outdoorsmen forced to survive in harsh conditions. Even after two years and making a success of his ranch, John felt inadequate, an Eastern transplant who still needed to become better adapted to western life. He projected confidence and it helped that he was a fast draw and an accurate shooter, but sometimes, when he had time to reflect over his life, he felt alone and disconnected.

His musings were interrupted by the arrival of the new rider. He dismounted an old and tired-looking horse. Before judging the man, John was outraged by the mistreated animal. A horse was a man's survival here in the wilderness and this one looked to be on its last prayers, skin and bones, and probably forced to run to the point of exhaustion.

The man was of an uncertain age, unkempt and dirty. What John disliked mostly were his shifty eyes and oily smile revealing gaps between his yellowed teeth.

“Howdy, folks. Do you mind if I warm these old bones by your fire?” he asked, taking note of the rifles they held close.

Yes, they minded. But a man could get lost far from a settlement, and until proven a danger, it was customary to help. Wayne returned as quietly as he’d left and, with an imperceptible shake of his head to Renard, confirmed that the rider was alone.

“Take a seat,” John invited him and Renard pushed toward him a tin half full with baked beans.

The man gobbled the beans like they were a special treat, a sign that he’d been hungry. Then he wiped his mouth on his sleeve and announced he was going to sleep on a pallet a few feet away from the fire.

Renard and Wayne wrapped themselves in blankets and lay down positioned to face the stranger. John took the first watch and quiet enveloped the camp.

He kept his eyes open and paid attention to any noise, but soon, he let his mind meander through memories of childhood with a loving and carefree father and an autocratic mother, who led with a strong will, both the family and the business she inherited from her own father. She had no understanding for the man she'd married, a pianist whose artistic soul and dreamy nature annoyed her to no end. She was still known as Miss Leticia Farrell and not Mrs. Gorman. After his father's passing, when John was twelve, his teenage years had been sad and lonely. He found solace in the western novels that he read with passion, giving free rein to the imagination. After ten years of trying to lead the business and butting heads with his mother, he decided he had enough and took a train west, eager for adventure. He was not naïve. He knew life was

hard in the west and full of dangers. But when the opportunity presented and he met a rancher willing to sell his land at a bargain price, he gambled for the first time in his life and gave the man almost all his savings in exchange for the deed to the ranch.

It hadn't been easy to turn the failing ranching operation into a successful one, but he did it and he had reasons to be proud. For the first time, he wondered what had driven Celia to go west. She obviously came from a wealthy family, despite not having money to continue her journey to San Francisco. It was likely that her parents wanted to marry her off and she'd rebelled. Was this the truth? Maybe he should ask her about it when he returned home.

A slight movement at the corner of his eye made him aware that the stranger was up. Assured that all in the camp were sleeping, including John who was the watch, the man got up slowly and went to rummage in John's saddle, the only one that was still on the horse.

John took the rifle and cocked it with a loud click. “Raise your hands where I can see them,” he said. The stranger obeyed and turned to John.

Renard opened his eyes, saw that John had the situation well in hand and closed them back. Wayne Dunbar sat up and pulling out his knife started to twirl it in his hand.

“Now see here, gents, I ain’t done nothing. I couldn’t sleep and wandered around,” the man argued, his eyes shifting assessing the situation.

“Who sent you?”

“No one sent me. What a question… I was traveling from Cody south to Colorado. I heard there is some more gold to be panned there. I thought I’d try my luck partnering with a man with a claim.”

The story could be true, but John was not convinced. “Go back to your pallet and keep your hands away from our horses,” he said reluctantly, lowering his rifle.

For a moment, he thought the man would do just that, but in a swift move, unexpected for a man his age and none too agile, the man vaulted onto John's horse and rode away fast. Or so he thought.

Annoyed, John rolled his eyes and then whistled sharply. People at his ranch knew better than to try to ride his stallion. The horse was not entirely tame and quite ornery. He only obeyed John and didn't suffer any other rider.

Despite the stranger's hard pull on the reins, the stallion returned to the camp, where rising on his hind legs, he threw the rider in the dirt.

"They used to hang horse thieves here in the west," Wayne commented.

"No, no. You can't do this," The man shouted. Standing up, he first tried to run on foot. Then he turned around and made the mistake to draw. John's gun cleared his holster faster and the man dropped to the ground.

"You'd think he had a death wish," Renard commented.

"Some people are plain stupid and don't know when to back down," Wayne added. "Too bad we couldn't find out if he came spying from the killers hidden up in the mountains. He did try to ride in that direction, not south where he claimed he wanted to go. And there is nothing in his saddle, except a few stolen things, a watch without much value, a brooch, and a woman's earring."

"I could be wrong, but I've seen the earring before. It belongs to one of the girls at Wilkes' saloon," Renard said.

The rest of the night was uneventful and in the morning they continued their ride north. The more they rode in that direction, the wide prairie narrowed and the landscape became rockier and hilly. The mountainous formation was more difficult to ride. Maybe this was not the right way, John wondered, although Renard seemed quite sure following the tracks.

He was watching a bird on a rock above them, when unexpectedly, Renard shouted, "Get down." Firing his rifle, he jumped down from his horse. "Get behind that rock. I'll cover you."

The attackers were somewhere on the opposite side of the passage.

"It's only a matter of time until they'll surround us," Renard observed recharging his rifle.

"Is this an ambush?" John asked him, checking his own guns.

"I don't think so. More like we stumbled upon them."

"Where is Wayne?"

"He crawled up there to eliminate the shooter from behind that rock. From down here, we have no chance to get him while we are an easy target for him."

A bullet ricocheted from the rock and whizzed past John's ear. He fired his rifle in the direction of the shooter hiding higher up, behind the rocks in front of them. He was reloading his rifle when a sharp cry alerted him that someone was hit. The shooter fell from the rock high above.

"Ha, Wayne nabbed him. I told you he was

good," Renard said with satisfaction reloading his Colt and firing again. "Bad news is - there are more than three hiding there."

One of the outlaws decided to run away and a horse with a rider came briefly in view before riding away fast.

"I'm going after him. Cover me," John shouted at Renard and whistling for his horse he vaulted in the saddle in one fluid movement, urging his horse forward. There was some distance between him and his prey, but the outlaw's horse was no match to John's nervous stallion. Soon he came closer. The outlaw sensing danger, turned around and fired his gun. John rode low, bent over his saddle and the bullet went wildly away.

He urged his horse faster. Then he uncoiled his lasso and just like he did in spring at round-up, he twirled it twice in the air and let it fly toward his prey. It worked and he felt like cheering up. He was a good cowboy, not a green easterner.

John pulled it tight and yanked it forcefully.

Unable to control his horse, the man fell with a jarring thud to the ground. The outlaw was dazed for a moment and it was enough for John to jump down and in one fast move to tie him up like a trussed turkey. He tossed him up over the saddle on the obediently waiting horse, while enduring the most vile swearing words he had ever heard.

He grabbed the bridle of the outlaw's horse and rode back to where he'd left his men.

CHAPTER 6

He found the other two ready to mount up and ride after him. The fight was over. Three outlaws were dead and one had escaped unfortunately – they reported, cheered up when they saw John's prisoner.

"Renard, are you sure these people who attacked us were the ones that shot Toby and his family? This man won't talk," John asked his foreman and trustful tracker.

"Yeah, they were the ones."

Wayne took out his Bowie knife. "I can make him talk."

John was tempted to let Wayne scare the outlaw, but in the end he gave up. Even under the threat to have his throat cut, the outlaw kept saying he didn't know the man who paid their gang to raid Toby's place and kill him, his sister and her child. He wouldn't hesitate to kill again. The way he saw it, it was a job he had to do. Probably he told the truth when he said he had no idea who was the person who paid them, or he feared that person too much to reveal who he was.

He was not too worried about going to jail and being tried for crimes. He assumed all the people he shot were dead. He didn't know that thanks to Renard, Toby was still alive and could identify him.

"All right, we'll take him to the sheriff," John said, eager to return home to his ranch. At least the weather was not unpleasantly cold and no early snowstorm was imminent.

They tied the outlaw to the saddle and rode back south where they came from. When the night was upon them, they stopped and made a campfire to eat whatever was left from what Cook had packed for them.

Warming near the fire, with a cup of hot coffee in hand, John remembered the conversation with Celia about giving people a chance to explain their acts before judging. "Why did you challenge Deputy McCarthy to a gunfight?" he asked Wayne, genuinely curious. The man newly hired by Renard seemed a tough hombre, but not a mindless gunslinger.

Surprised by the question, Wayne paused cleaning his knife and pondered if to answer or not. Like all westerners, he was a private man who considered it was no one's business why he did what he did. Free as a bird, he was not accountable to anyone and he liked it this way. But sharing a meal and a campfire after a gunfight, it mellowed a body a tad and made him feel more open. He shrugged. "He killed my father."

The answer was so unexpected that John's jaw dropped. "McCarthy killed your father?" he questioned in disbelief. "It must have been a mistake, surely." Although McCarthy was not known to make any mistakes when he pointed his gun. He was accurate and lethal.

"No, it was not a mistake," Wayne said. Now that he'd opened his mouth and told them more than they needed to know, he might as well tell them the whole sordid story. "My father was a gun for hire, very arrogant. He liked to believe he was the fastest draw in all Texas. Although quite young, McCarthy had a reputation as being a shrewd card player and the best gunfighter that there was. So, my father decided to prove once and for all that he was the best and fastest."

"Ah, a vain ambition that brings no glory," Renard added his own thoughts, while filling their tin cups with more of the hot liquid.

"True," Wayne agreed. "Especially because he mistook another for McCarthy. He shot and killed an innocent man. Only then, McCarthy revealed who he was, accepted the challenge, shot and killed my father."

"If you knew all this, then why did you challenge McCarthy to a gunfight?" John asked. "He didn't mean to kill your father. He had to."

"At the time, it seemed the thing to do," Wayne explained cryptically. After a brief moment, he added, "He never married my mother. She raised me alone, earning money the best she could, cooking at the tavern, taking in laundry, cleaning houses. He used to come once every three-four months, when he was in need of a respite, or of money. The child I was then, refused to see him for the no-good man that he was. I thought the world started with him. He was my idol and I wanted to make him… I don't know what I wanted, stupid child that I was."

"Yeah. I can see how you needed to identify with him and to think he was the best. A boy needs this kind of assurance. I understand," John told him. "But, what about later, when you saw how worthless he was?"

"I had a score to settle with myself," was all Wayne said and wrapping himself in his blanket, closed his eyes, a sign that the conversation was over.

John sighed. There was more to Wayne Dunbar than he'd presumed at first. He was a complex man and had a lot of demons to chase. John turned to Renard, but his foreman had taken first watch and with his rifle on his knee and his eyes glued to their tied-up prisoner, he was puffing his pipe.

Renard woke him up around midnight to take

over the watch. "It's quiet," he said. Then he bent closer and whispered, "Maybe too quiet. He didn't move under that blanket, but I have a bad feel about him," he inclined his head toward the unmoving figure of the outlaw. "My left eye is twitching. Take care."

Like any man who'd lived most of his life in wilderness, Renard was used to sense danger before he saw or heard it, and he had premonitions that most times proved true.

John touched his gun and pulled his holster to make it more easy accessible, but he knew he won't use it tonight. It was important to get the outlaw alive to the sheriff and to discover the identity of the man who had ordered the senseless killings. He owed it to Toby and his sister.

Renard's warning proved to be true. An hour after midnight, John saw the outlaw silently moving under the blanket, a sign that somehow he'd managed to cut his ties. Probably he had a knife in his boot that they had missed when they'd searched him. He

crawled slowly toward the horses.

He had his hand on the bridle of John's horse, judging it correctly to be the fastest of the three, and not knowing of its temperamental nature.

"Stay right there," John said, raising his rifle and coming closer. For a moment, it was like a repeat of the previous night and he wondered if it was going to end the same.

But this outlaw was not as predictable as the other one and he had no gun. Pretending to raise his hands up, he turned fast and threw the knife at John. John jumped to the side, but not fast enough and he had to deflect the knife with the butt of his rifle. Instantly, the man was on him trying to yank the rifle from him. John lost his balance, but not his grip on the rifle.

They fell to the ground, fighting for the rifle. The man rolled on top, and applied pressure on the rifle to John's throat. Wayne and Renard had been awakened by the whole ruckus and John knew they would intervene in the last moment if needed. For now, it was his pride to succeed without help in a one on one fight.

With a mighty effort, he twisted to the side sitting up, pulling on the rifle. Then he let it go abruptly and in that second of confusion and hesitation from his opponent, John applied a left fist to the other man's jaw followed by a right one in rapid succession. Boxing lessons from his college days came in handy and the outlaw fell to the ground, releasing his hold on the rifle.

When he came back to life, shaking his head and gingerly touching his jaw, John hunkered down near him and this time he cocked his gun to his head in unmistakable threat.

Renard threw him a rope. Placing his gun back in the holster, John tied him up again, making sure the binds were tighter and grabbing the rifle from the ground.

"Not bad for an Eastern man," Renard chuckled, while Wayne was looking at him from under his brows, playing with the newly confiscated knife, suggesting how he would have dealt with his opponent in a fight. It was all the recognition John was going to get. Not that he needed anything other than that.

When they arrived home next day, the men came out from wherever they had work to do and Celia and Cook were waiting on the porch. It was good to be welcomed home by a pretty woman, John admitted, forgetting that he'd sworn to remain a crusty old bachelor forever.

He dismounted his horse and looked at his men who surrounded them. "The rest of Toby's killers are dead. They attacked us and we shot them. We still don't know who ordered it. This one tried to run away and we caught him. Take him to the barn and tie him to a post there," John said pointing at their prisoner. "Tomorrow we'll take him to the sheriff."

"Aw, Boss, let us string him from the rafters," one of the men asked.

"Or from that thick branch yonder," another suggested.

"No mercy, like they didn't show for Toby."

Lest he was going to have a lynching in his own yard, John had to intervene. "We're better men than that, I'd like to think. Justice will be done, but by the law. Now take him in the barn, as I said," he ordered with as much authority as he could muster. When the grumbling men dispersed to do as he requested, John asked Renard in a lower voice, "Do you think they'll do as I asked?"

Renard nodded. "Oh, sure, they'll do it. They'll rough him up a little, but they'll have him ready tomorrow to be taken to town."

On the porch, Celia smiled at them. "I'm glad you're back home safe, Cousin John."

That gave him pause, until he remembered they were supposed to be cousins. "I'm sorry if you found life on a ranch boring, Celia. Unfortunately, tomorrow we have to take that man to town, so you'll be all alone again." After seeing the outlaw in jail, he was going to think about this and what to do about her.

"I don't find anything boring here. On the contrary, everything is new and fascinating to me," she assured him honestly and not because she wanted to be polite. "As for tomorrow, I'd like to go to town with you to send a telegram to Aunt Clara in San Francisco."

That stopped him short. He had to transport the outlaw to town safely, and couldn't worry about Celia's safety too.

"Let's go inside to talk," Cook suggested wisely.

But once inside, the issue didn't look any easier to resolve. What to do about Celia? "Listen, the easiest way for me would be to buy you a train ticket to California. Perhaps another man in my place would do just that. But I can't in good conscience to let you go alone on the train, a young woman unaccompanied, prey to all the ruffians aboard. No, I can't do it."

"You don't have to. You see, I've decided to visit here for a while, Cousin John. Either way, if I stay or leave, I'm indebted to you. So I've decided to stay and let Aunt Clara know where I am and ask her to send some money. It's the best solution." She beamed at him. "Meanwhile, we'll see what the next day has in store for us."

"Exactly so," Renard added his own opinion, snatching a warm biscuit from the basket on the table. "Your cousin is pleasing to the eyes. Why not stay here? And who knows what the good Lord has decided for us."

CHAPTER 7

It seemed so simple the night before. Take the tied-up prisoner with the wagon to the Sheriff's Office and while in town, go to the bank and to the Land Management Office. Also go to the mercantile to buy Cook what she wrote on her list. And if Celia wanted to go to town to send a telegram to her aunt, she was welcome to travel with them. That's what John thought yesterday.

Today… it was not so simple.

"What's on your mind, Boss?" Renard joined him on the porch, munching a last biscuit from this morning's breakfast. Every man had his own weakness and in Renard's case, he couldn't resist Cook's biscuits.

"I'm trying to figure out how to do everything I need to do this morning. There is no way I can take Celia, a delicate Eastern lady, in the same wagon with the outlaw. Then, also in her presence, we have to tell the sheriff about the gruesome murder of Toby's sister and her son. Not to mention that in the Sheriff's Office occasionally come and go all kind of dubious characters, card players, drunkards, saloon girls."

"Miss Celia doesn't look so delicate. Pretty as a picture and well-mannered, yes, but not fragile to shatter at the sight of a saloon girl," Renard commented, shaking off the crumbs from his shirt and taking his pipe out of his pocket.

John ignored his words and continued his line of thinking. "On top of this, I have to watch the prisoner not to escape like he tried before, and while at the Sheriff's Office, to make sure Wayne is not in the mood to drag the deputy in the street for another gunfight. You'd better believe that this time McCarthy won't be so merciful." His eyes fell on the colorful buggy, which looked like a peacock with its blue top and bright pink fringes. "And I have to take the buggy back to Timmy at the train depot. How can I drive both the wagon and the buggy in the same time?"

Renard's eyes sparkled, amused at his

predicament. “You can’t. But between the two of us, we can drive the wagon and make sure the outlaw doesn’t escape and is safely delivered to the sheriff.”

John nodded. “I thought so me too. And Celia will have to wait for another day to send her telegram.”

“No. If Cousin Celia wants to come to town, then she should be able to do it anytime. You can’t keep her in the house. It’s only that many biscuits she can burn trying to master the fine art of cooking.” They both rolled their eyes in agreement. Celia needed to be kept away from the kitchen. “At least she comes from a rich family and can afford to hire a cook,” Renard concluded.

“How do you know she’s rich? She didn’t have two pennies in her reticule when she fainted of hunger.”

Renard waved his hand. “Just look at her. You can see she’s quality. Granted she doesn’t know practical things for a woman in the west, like cooking, but she can use a rifle and she’s not a shrinking violet to be afraid to do it. Did she tell you anything about herself?"

It was pointless to pretend that Celia was his cousin. The old fox knew better and also John was assured that Renard was not going to talk in town about this business. "No, she didn't and I didn't ask. I don't tell people details about my private life either."

From the barn, Wayne came out with his horse saddled ready to go to town. Renard pointed his pipe at him. "Here is your answer. Let Wayne drive Celia to town in the buggy and send Timmy, the clerk, some money for using his vehicle a while longer."

John frowned. "I don't know Wayne well enough to trust him to take care of Celia. As long as she's in my care, I have to ensure her safety."

"There is no better man to keep her safe than Wayne. He's ready to fight any outlaw to protect Celia and not just because he was ordered to do so. He has a deep respect for women," Renard argued.

As much as he disliked the idea of letting another man accompany Celia to town, John had to admit that this would make his life easier and he could finish faster everything he had to do today. Not to mention he was not going to drive the colorful buggy to town and become a laughingstock. "Very well. Wayne, could you drive Cousin Celia to town today?"

Just then Celia walked out on the porch, picture-pretty in her traveling dress, freshly cleaned and pressed, wearing a jaunty hat, ornate with silk flowers and ribbons, perched at an angle on top of her curly dark hair. She was twirling a lacy parasol, totally useless in the late October sun, unless she planned to use it as a weapon on a too daring townsman. She didn't have it when she'd left the train station so John assumed that she'd searched his attic while they were chasing the gang. He didn't mind. In fact, he hadn't done it after he'd bought the property from the Millers. He'd simply had no time and had postponed this chore.

His face unreadable as usual, Wayne stopped and looked at her considering. Then he nodded curtly and said, "I'll go to harness the horses to the buggy."

"Wayne," John shouted after him. "Renard assured me that you're trustful. I believe him. See that no harm will come to Cousin Celia while in your care or I'll personally hunt you down. And unlike McCarthy, I'm not going to be shy to face you in a direct gunfight. I'll let you see then who's faster."

Renard turned to him. "No need for threats, Boss. Wayne is reliable."

The two men were not paying attention to him. They were engaged in a battle of wills for no other reason at all, except pride and vanity, like two roosters in the yard.

John had no idea why he doubted Wayne's ability to take care of Celia and why it rankled him to let Wayne escort her to town, despite being so convenient. Wayne, his honor questioned and not one to take threats easy, stopped and facing John he touched his gun in the holster like saying, 'I'm ready.'

Ignoring the tense undercurrents that flew between the two men, Celia stepped forward and smiled graciously. “I’m sure I’ll be perfectly safe with Mr. Dunbar, cousin. How thoughtful of you to spare him in order to drive me to town. Although I could have driven this elegant buggy myself, how difficult can it be after all? Or I could stay home and help Cook to make some more of those delicious biscuits.”

“No,” Renard objected. “I mean, no need for you to stay home if you have business in town. Wayne will be more than happy to drive you.” He raised an eyebrow at Wayne.

“Yes, of course,” Wayne muttered, still staring at John daring him to continue their dispute.

John relaxed his stance. Whatever his foreman knew about Wayne it made Renard trust his loyalty without question. So John had to accept that. “Very well. Go harness the horses to the buggy. And tell Mathias and the men to bring the prisoner to the wagon and to check that he is tied securely.”

He watched as Wayne assisted Celia to climb in the buggy and clenched his fists when the man took a seat near her and drove her away. He only hoped that Celia knew to handle that parasol as well as the rifle at her feet. He didn't know why he had this hostility toward the man recently hired by Renard. He'd proved very useful in the chase after the murderous gang and Renard believed in him. John couldn't even say that his inner sense of danger warned him against Wayne Dunbar, because it didn't.

Shrugging this off, he checked again that the outlaw's binds were strong, ignored the heinous looks he sent his way and climbed in the driver's seat. Renard climbed in the back, near the man, to watch him all the way to town.

After leaving Mathias in charge until he returned and giving him instructions, John took the reins and they were off to town.

"I still worry about Celia," John muttered after a while.

"Did you ask yourself why?" Renard said from behind.

Not expecting a comment John was surprised. "Because she's my guest, naturally. I feel responsible for her and her safety."

"Nonsense," Renard scoffed. "If my great-aunt Winifred were your guest, you wouldn't fret so much, I bet."

"You don't have a great-aunt Winifred."

"That's beside the point. You built a good ranch here. It's time to find yourself a fine woman to share life with."

John experienced again the old feel of longing for what he couldn't have. "How can you even suggest it? You know how much I loved Esmé Richardson." At the time, Renard had been working for Esmé's brother, Lloyd and he was aware of what had been going on.

"Loved – past tense. It's time you moved on. Life went on. You should too." Renard advised him philosophically. Although he was not much older than John, sometimes he treated his employer like a youngster in need of advice. And John didn't accept this from anyone else, but Renard.

He sighed deeply. "You know why I can't. Tell

me at least that she's alive and well," he asked Renard. His beloved Esmé had vanished from home in mysterious conditions. People in town talked that the beautiful Esmé, in love with an outlaw, took her own life after her lover was killed by a bounty hunter. The family claimed that she moved permanently to live in Chicago where she had an aunt. Outlaw or not, John had asked her to marry him and she had flatly refused him. Yet, after more than a year, he still couldn't forget her. His blond, blue-eyed angel. There would never be any other woman like her.

Renard kept silent for a long moment and John thought he wouldn't answer him. It was like the whole Richardson family and their people took a vow to keep silent when asked about Esmé. "She's alive and happy," Renard said finally in a low voice. "And that's all I'm going to say. It's time for you to move on and what better way than with this pretty filly, who fell into your lap."

"No, no," John protested without even considering. "She's not suitable for life at the ranch.

You yourself said she is not what a rancher is looking for in a wife."

"She might surprise you. She didn't faint in horror when you were attacked by the squatters, did she? She grabbed the gun and shot at them."

"She… she's not… blond. I like sweet blond women, with blue eyes…"

"…and named Esmé," Renard filled in for him. "It ain't gonna happen," he added flatly. "And if you dither too much, another one will steal Celia from under your nose. Don't forget women are scarce in the west, good women even more so, and Celia is beautiful and wealthy."

"She wants to go to San Francisco to visit her aunt. I bet she'd be horrified if I asked her to stay and marry me. She'd refuse me." Like another did before and shredded his heart to pieces with her rejection. John was not going to risk his heart and his pride again.

"There is more to this visit than she said. She left in haste, without money or a large trunk full of

whatever women consider necessary. She left because she had to, and I bet she'd like a place to call home if Philadelphia is no longer safe for her. For whatever her reasons. You think about it."

CHAPTER 8

It was a pleasant October day and for a while Celia admired with curiosity the vast empty space around her, so wild and untamed, so different than the familiar places back East. Her companion was content to hold the reins and drive in silence.

She measured him from under her dark lashes. He was rugged and compared to the polite and elegant dandies in Philadelphia he couldn't be called handsome. Yet he projected an aura of strength and even danger that made him interestingly attractive. He was as untamed as the nature surrounding them and had only a thin veneer of civilization, unlike John Gorman who'd been raised and educated in the East and was more polished.

"You're quiet, Mr. Dunbar," she said when she couldn't stand the silence any longer. Besides, she was intrigued by her travel companion.

"Hmm, men don't talk much," was all he muttered under his breath.

She straightened the folds of her skirt primly and continued in the same tone. "Cook said you are a gunslinger and a very dangerous man who should be avoided by young innocent women. That's what she said." Of course, she was not so naïve and innocent as Cook assumed and in this case she decided to take the tiger by the tail and find out for herself the truth about him.

Wayne could bet that in the three to four days she had been cooped up in the house with Cook, the old woman had told her all that she knew about everyone on the ranch and in town and some stories she assumed were true, plus her own personal opinion about everything and everyone. Add to this that Cook never liked Wayne from the first day she'd laid eyes on him. And why would she? No one ever liked him and he was used to people's disapproval of him as long as they didn't overtly insult him or interfere with his plans. "Cook was right. You'd better keep away from men like me, Miss Celia."

"Nonsense. Cousin John wouldn't have

allowed you to drive me to town if he thought I was in any danger from you and in general I like to make my own opinion," she said firmly. "Why did you challenge the deputy to a gunfight? Cook said you wanted revenge. Is it true?"

It would be so simple to say that yes, he'd wanted revenge. But it was not the truth, not the whole truth. "Ten years ago, McCarthy shot my father dead in a saloon gunfight. But I've always known that he was right to do so. I didn't know all the details of that fight, but I came to realize that my father was a selfish, vain man. It was only a matter of time before he ended up the way he did." Frustrated, he stopped talking. It was the second time in as many days that he talked to strangers about his personal life and struggles. What was wrong with him? No one could understand what he felt.

Gently Celia placed a hand on his arm. "Then what happened?"

Almost against his will, Wayne started to talk. "It is a story about revenge, but not against

McCarthy. For two years, I chased a man who'd committed a crime down in Texas. Now I finally found him as leader of a gang of robbers holed up in the mountains south of here. One night, he came into the saloon and we met at the card table."

"He cheated," Celia guessed.

"No. He didn't need to. He intimidated and bullied the others to give him the pot on the table regardless if he had a winning hand or not. I said no and he drew on me. I was faster and I shot him dead. I'm a killer, Miss Celia. Cook was right."

She took a deep breath before asking in the same gentle voice. "What did he do?"

"He beat to death a young Mexican woman who worked at a cantina and he threw her body in a ravine there near the border," he explained.

"Was she your sweetheart?" Celia asked in a barely audible voice.

After a long while, Wayne shook his head. "No, ma'am. I never had a sweetheart. She was just a poor girl, who helped me when I was in need. I promised that I'd take care of her. She didn't ask for anything, but I considered her my responsibility. And I failed her. The only thing I could do was to get justice for her. Too little, too late," he remarked with bitterness in his voice.

"Sometimes despite doing our best, we are helpless. Bad things happen to the ones we love."

They continued to drive in silence, both of them caught up in their thoughts. Until Celia realized he didn't answer her initial question and she was persistent. "This story had nothing to do with the deputy, so why did you challenge him and so publicly in the middle of town?"

"I see Cook gave you all the details," he said. "I can't explain very well why I did it. After shooting that bandit, I felt strange. All the purpose that had driven me on for two years was no more. I had an odd feeling of uselessness. I didn't know what to do with myself. On a dare, I asked McCarthy out."

"But you knew he was lightening fast. You could have been killed." Celia looked at him worrying her lower lip between her teeth. When understanding dawned, her eyes widened. "Good Lord, you knew that and still wanted to have a gunfight. You… wanted to die?"

"No, I didn't. It was more like a dare - I told you - in a moment when I felt unsure what to do with my life and not caring about it much. Am I good, better than McCarthy or not? I was willing to prove myself," he answered, frustrated that he couldn't explain better and maybe because deep down he didn't understand fully himself why he had done it. It had seemed the thing to do at the time.

"You mean like those silly men who want the fame of being the fastest gun in the west?"

"I don't know. Probably I'm no better than my father. Now are you satisfied for finding out the ugly truth? You couldn't leave it alone, could you?"

No, she couldn't. Celia shook her head. "You are a good man. You were confused, caught between the need to love your father and slowly understanding that he was not worthy of your admiration. Then the grief for your friend, who died so tragically, affected your judgment and made revenge the purpose of your life."

If she wanted to believe he was better than he truly was, then who was he to contradict her. With relief, he saw in the distance the first houses at the edge of town. "Here we are. We'll go to the train depot first. The telegraph office is nearby."

Distracted, Celia looked interested at the buildings and stores in town especially the Trabing Commercial Co. store, a large building with a variety of merchandise.

Their fringed buggy attracted people's interest, and some of them waved friendly. If Wayne was chagrined or embarrassed by getting that much attention, he didn't show. Did he regret confessing the truth? Probably. He kept a stony face and he drove the buggy in silence the rest of the way. Celia tried to change the subject to a more neutral subject, but not being able to coax him out of his morose mood, she gave up for the moment and preferred to look around.

Wayne stopped the buggy in front of the train station. He was helping Celia to climb down from the seat when he heard a mocking voice behind him, "Lookee here, boys, what fancy pink fringes."

Ah, a good fight would be great, just what he needed in his dark mood. Unfortunately, he was with Celia and while he didn't care what others thought of him, he had to protect her, not only from ruffians like these three tipsy cowboys leering at her, but also from the sight of a violent fight. Gently reared ladies like her were not used to seeing the ugly rough side of life.

He left her up on the seat and turned to face the three cowboys. He touched his holster suggestively and tried to reason with them. "Move along boys before I decide that I find you offensive and make mincemeat of you. You don't want to make me mad."

The taller of them looked at him, then at his companions and decided that they had the advantage. "Who are you to threaten us? The pretty lady might want some better company than you. She's welcome to come with us." And saying this, he took a step forward and wiggled his brows at Celia. Then he extended his hand to her or to touch her, Wayne was not sure. Resigned that he had a fight brewing and it was unavoidable if he wanted to protect Celia, he threw a fist in the cowboy's soft belly. His opponent went down like a stone, falling in a heap on the ground.

After a moment of stunned pause, the second one came charging at Wayne head first like an enraged bull. "You killed my brother," he roared.

Wayne barely moved aside to avoid him. The force of the hit shook the buggy and the second cowboy fell near his companion dazed. Wayne looked up to see if Celia was all right, only to find the seat of the buggy empty. He turned and saw that she'd jumped down on the other side and now she was hitting the third ruffian with her parasol. A lethal weapon indeed, Wayne thought and before he could intervene she poked the man in the chest with the pointed tip.

Wayne stepped forward afraid of a violent reaction from the now angry cowboy. This saved his life as a bullet grazed the side of the buggy right where he stood before. In a blink of an eye, he drew his gun and fired in the direction from where the bullet had been shot.

Across the street, at the second floor he saw a slight movement behind the open window in the darkness inside. Then it was quiet and he knew that whoever had shot at him was no longer there. He wanted to run to catch him, but he couldn't leave Celia here alone. He doubted the three drunk cowboys were connected to the shooter, although they had been used as a diversion to keep Wayne there longer.

Meanwhile, the third cowboy touched his own gun, but seeing the fast way Wayne was using his, changed his mind. He gave a hand to the other two to get up and to move away on wobbly legs, giving a wide berth to Celia and her lethal parasol.

Assured that Celia was safe, Wayne looked

again at the open window from the top floor at the building across the street. Had he been the target of the gunman and for what reason? Not that he didn't have a lot of enemies all over the West who wanted him dead, because he had plenty. Or perhaps the shooter had confused him with John Gorman who was seen driving the colorful buggy when he'd been in town last.

Wayne looked at Celia who was now straightening her dress and rearranging her hat that looked so dignified that no one would ever imagine her in the middle of a fray. She was twirling her parasol coquettishly, looking every bit the elegant, subdued lady of quality that she was.

CHAPTER 9

A train leaving the station whistled loudly, making the horses nervous. Timmy, the clerk from the train depot came running, still carrying his signaling lantern.

"Mr. Dunbar, are you all right?" he asked. "I couldn't come sooner. I had to assist the train's departure." He frowned looking after the three troublemakers. "I know them. Isaiah and his brother work for Rancher Mallory. The other one is new in town. He used to hang out at Tom Wilkes' saloon. Never-do-wells all three of them."

"This rancher, Mallory, hires unreliable people like them?" Wayne asked, studying the damage the bullet had done to the buggy.

Timmy shrugged. "His ranch is west of town. Mallory can be seen playing cards at the saloon from time to time. I guess he met them there."

"Tell me, Timmy, who lives in the building across the street?"

"No one, sir. It was vacant since the saddle maker moved into a larger space on 2nd Street. Now he rents it to merchants who need some storage space close to the railway station. Even Tom Wilkes used to store some of his liquor here until one night robbers broke in and left with some of his bottles."

"Is it locked?"

Timmy lifted his cap and scratched his head. "Every merchant brings his own locks. Now, I think it's not locked. There is only a piano inside and who would bother to steal a piano?"

"A piano!" Celia exclaimed. Until then, she had waited patiently near the buggy, listening to their talk.

"Yes, ma'am. You see, this summer Rancher Mallory married Cora Lynn Turner. No one thought Cora Lynn would get married again, after banker Turner caught her gambling upstairs at the saloon and divorced her. Why Mallory married her, no one knows." Wayne rolled his eyes bored. Timmy was a great guy, but he had a penchant for gossip. Wayne opened his mouth to interrupt him when the next words caught his attention. "Cora Lynn ordered a piano for her new home, Mallory's house. And not a regular one as you see in church, but a huge concert instrument. It took six strong cowboys to move it from the train here in the street and when they tried to lift it in a wagon. The piano damaged the wagon and they gave up. Rancher Mallory moved it inside the building here across the street." Timmy stopped talking and looked at the place, then at Wayne. "It is possible he sent the three cowboys to try to remove the piano."

Wayne would have loved to go inside and see for himself what was going on there, especially at the upper floor. But again, taking care of Celia was a priority.

"I see you like the buggy," Timmy changed the subject smiling at Celia.

"Oh, yes. It's splendid. I haven't seen in all Philadelphia such a fine-looking vehicle," she answered.

Timmy beamed at her. “Feel free to use it anytime, ma’am. Ladies in particular like it.”

“About that…,” Wayne interfered. “…John Gorman sent you some money for a longer use of the buggy. His cousin Celia here will visit us for a longer time,” he inclined his head toward her. Then he gave some money to the surprised young man.

Timmy knew that Celia had just met John on the train and was not his cousin, but he didn’t say or contradict Wayne. He tried to refuse the money politely. “No need, sir. I told Mr. Gorman that I don’t charge the locals for using it.”

Wayne patted him over the pocket of his coat. “Take it, Timmy. Business is business. Now lead us to the telegraph’s office. Miss Celia wants to send a telegram to her aunt in San Francisco.”

After the telegraph operator assured them he’d send it right away, they left the office and helping Celia climb back in the buggy, Wayne drove a few blocks away to the dressmaker. The investigation into who shot at him and why would have to wait for later.

"John Gorman wanted you to order a couple more dresses and whatever else you ladies need. He'll pay for it," Wayne told her.

Embarrassed, Celia bit her lower lip. "Oh, I couldn't accept his money."

A practical man all his life, Wayne couldn't understand her hesitation. "Due to probably the haste when you left home, you find yourself without clothes, except what you have on, and without money. You have to accept Cousin John's offer of help." She had tears in her eyes and he felt like a brute for bullying her so. "Look, you need this and you can repay him when you'll be able to do it."

Gorman had placed him in a difficult situation. What did Wayne know about escorting a lady of quality or talking with her? He hired as a gunslinger, not as polite escort. He breathed easier when she nodded in agreement.

They stopped in front of the entrance and Wayne pointed at the dress presented on a mannequin in the window of the shop. "That thing," he said pointing to the prominent bustle in the back of the dress that was all the rage in the East. "That thing might not be so practical for life on the ranch."

Celia giggled behind her hand. "This dress is the latest fashion and I'm glad to see an outfit like this here."

Wayne snapped his mouth shut and opened the door for her. What did he know about fashion anyhow? He hoped Gorman didn't want him to act as fashion adviser. He could just as well quit right now.

The owner of the shop, Emily Richardson, wife of their neighbor Lloyd was equally amused by his uneasiness to be in a woman's world. She led him to a dainty chair and offered him tea and a bunch of magazines about ranching and some newspapers. Soon he was entranced in reading and Celia was taken in the back room by the dressmaker to take her measurements and to choose what she wanted.

After half an hour, Wayne called her and said that she can take her time to talk about fashion. He had an errand to do and he'd be back in an hour.

He left the store, placed his hat on and breathed deeply the clean October air. He was at the corner when he heard Celia calling him.

"Wayne, wait for me. I want to go with you," she said coming to a halt near him.

Why couldn't the pesky female be interested in dresses and give him an hour of respite? "It's not possible, Miss Celia. Where I'm going is not a proper place for ladies."

"Come on, Wayne," she tried to cajole him. "I don't think you're going to the saloon in the middle of the day. Or… to a house of ill repute," she hesitated before saying the last words.

"You shouldn't even know that such places exist," he admonished her and resigned, he walked back where he left the buggy. "It's not an immoral place where I'm going," he finally said, starting to drive the buggy.

"Show me what it is then."

He shook his head. "It's still not a place for

ladies. It's dirty and even dangerous." But he drove on, not very far on the 2nd Street and stopped the buggy in front of a general repair shop. In front of it, there were three bicycles.

"Bicycles?" Celia said surprised. "You like them? Cousin John thinks they are funny and they can't replace the horses."

"He's right. Bicycles can't, but maybe one day something will. Come," he said extending his hand to help her down. "And be careful not to snag your skirts on some sharp corners."

He guided her to another building, very dingy and industrial looking. Celia had to hold on to her skirts not to get dirty and to step gingerly among the many objects lying around. In the middle of the large room, there was a buggy in process of being assembled.

Celia was disappointed. She didn't know what she'd expected, but this was not it. A buggy, really? She looked around her hoping the place hid some mystery or some exciting object. Nothing.

A young man, maybe sixteen years of age, came to shake hands with Wayne. His hands were still dirty despite wiping them in a dirty cloth, so now Wayne's hands were stained with the oily material. They looked at each other and laughed. Celia didn't find this hilarious at all. She stepped back just in case the young man decided to shake her hand too. She was relieved when he only inclined his head politely. "Ma'am."

"Celia, this young fellow is Elmer Lovejoy," Wayne told her while he washed his hands at a utilitarian sink nearby. "Elmer, Celia is John Gorman's cousin from Philadelphia, who is visiting us. She wanted to see where I was going and I bet she's regretting her curiosity now."

"No, I'm not. It's just that I've seen buggies before. In fact, we were driving a very nice one rented from the train station clerk."

"Really? Wayne, are you driving the pink fringed vehicle?" Elmer chortled amused.

That irritated Celia. She was very fond of the

colorful buggy. "I'll have you know that buggy is very nice and it's working. This one doesn't." she pointed toward the vehicle in the middle of the room.

"No, ma'am. It doesn't and it will not for quite some time until I succeed to solve all the issues that I have now and put all the parts together," Elmer explained.

Intrigued, she came closer to take a better look. "Why? What's wrong with it?"

Wayne touched the buggy reverently. "It will work without horses. The time will come when people will drive buggies without the need of a horse. It's only a matter of time, sooner than you think."

"Without horses? It's not possible."

"Why not?" Elmer asked her. "Think of the train locomotive."

"But it's not the same. The train has a huge engine that pushes it forward."

Elmer grimaced. "It can be done on a smaller scale. I just have to figure out how."

He talked some technical details with Wayne,

then Celia wished him luck and to her great relief they were off.

"Do you believe in his crazy ideas about buggy travel without horses?" she asked Wayne when they were back in the colorful buggy with horses, driving through town.

"That's why I came back to town. For Elmer and his ideas. He's young, but he'll succeed. Mark my words. And he's not the only one in the country trying to build a horseless vehicle. We are close to the turn of the century and there is a rush toward inventions that will change our way of living. Some, we can't even imagine. Elmer has a vision and he has given me a glance into how it will be. But above all other considerations, young as he is, he has a purpose in life and I envy him for this."

CHAPTER 10

By the time he reached the Sheriff's Office, John was in a bad mood. Instead of Celia's gracious presence, he had to bear the most foul language that he had ever heard, as the outlaw was cursing and threatening them all the way. When they were close to town even Renard had enough and he was not fazed by rough words or explicit curses. He pulled out his knife and told the prisoner that if he didn't shut up, he's going to get a knife to the gut and then he'd wish the posse would catch and hang him. One look at Renard assured him that the foreman was dead-serious. It quieted him down and stopped any attempt at jumping from the wagon to escape.

John found Sheriff Bill Monroe sitting behind his desk reading aloud some article in a newspaper and both he and Deputy McCarthy were laughing at whatever funny material was there. John was in no mood for being amused, despite this being a nice sunny October day and people in Laramie were smiling friendly.

“I brought you a prisoner, Sheriff,” he told Monroe, signaling for Renard to bring in their man.

The sheriff stood up and looked the outlaw over. He nodded satisfied. “Ah, Blind Ted, we meet again.”

Renard frowned. “He ain’t blind. I wish he were.”

“It’s his gang name. He has a glass eye and can’t see well on the left side.”

“You know him?” John asked.

“Sure. He’s on half a dozen Wanted posters. An old patron of the Federal Prison here in Laramie. What did he do this time?”

“Glass eye or not, he and his partners shot Toby and his family and killed his sister, Becky and her little boy. A senseless murder of innocent people,” John said.

The sheriff, who’d seen his share of killings in his life as a lawman, was taken aback. “It can’t be robbery. Toby was a poor man. And why kill a woman and a child?"

"I ain't kilt no one," the outlaw protested.

Deputy McCarthy took the keys to the cell from a peg and pushed him forward. The outlaw let out a string of curse words. "Watch your tongue if you don't want to swallow it accidentally," the deputy said unimpressed and locked him in a jail cell in the back.

"He was one of the three who attacked Toby's cabin. Toby recognized him."

"Toby's alive?"

"Yes, but barely. Four Fingers thinks he'll make it."

The sheriff nodded. "Then he's in good hands. He'll survive. Tell me what happened. Don't leave out any details."

John took a seat, accepted gratefully the cup of hot coffee offered by Jeremiah, the sheriff's volunteer helper and sometimes deputy in charge of the office when no one was around. Then John started talking about his travel to Kansas City and what happened when he came back. He thought first to leave out Celia's story, but people in town were bound to find out anyhow, so he mentioned her as a cousin visiting from Philadelphia. "...One of the outlaws escaped, but Renard is sure he was not one of the three who attacked Toby. And of course, there is the man who ordered the murders, as Toby suspected, the one connected to his sister, Becky, possibly the boy's father."

The sheriff pondered all this. "The woman was frightened to death by this man and didn't reveal his name not even to her brother and now it's too late. I doubt I can find his face among the Wanted men. It looks like he was a respectable citizen in the eyes of the townfolks. Of course, he could be a member of a gang of outlaws also. Too bad Becky didn't name him."

Then John remembered another detail. "Or maybe she tried to, in the last moment. When Renard found them, she clutched this in her hand." He took out of his pocket the silver coin on the broken chain.

"Wayne Dunbar thinks he saw it at a card table in the saloon. One of the players was twirling it in his hand. That's why he remembers it." He set the coin on the sheriff's desk.

The sheriff looked at it and shrugged. "It doesn't say anything to me."

Deputy McCarthy however, raised an eyebrow and then nodded. "It triggers some memory to me. It was on one of the tables, but I can't say who placed it there. I was not playing. Dunbar was, although both of us were focused on one man and his hirelings and couldn't allow our attention to be diverted elsewhere. That's how it is when a gunfight is imminent, if you were wondering why neither of us has a better recollection of what happened at a neighboring table."

"It's all right. I'll ask at the saloon. Maybe Tom Wilkes or one of the girls has seen it before." John pocketed the coin and rose to leave. Then he remembered one more thing he wanted to say. "Deputy, Renard thinks Wayne Dunbar is a trustworthy fellow and he hired him. I thought you should know that he's back in town, in case he decides to challenge you again. He doesn't seem to me to be a hotheaded gunfighter, always ready to draw. On the contrary, the few days spent with him chasing the outlaws proved he was reliable. But… one can never know. Why is he back?"

"Good question," McCarthy answered. "I thought he'd left town for good. His memories of the days spent here are not exactly pleasant. But I have a feeling he didn't come back with the intention of challenging me again. Anyhow, thanks for warning me."

John touched his hat in salute and left the office. He was followed by Renard who took the reins of the horses to drive the wagon. "Hop in, Boss," he said looking at John who had stopped on the boardwalk.

John waved him away. "You go to the mercantile to buy what Cook wrote on that paper. I have to go to the bank and to local office of the

Bureau of Land Management. I'll meet you later."

At the bank, he checked that the money he got for the cattle sold in Kansas City had been transferred and deposited in his account. Then he went to the Bureau of Land Management and checked some records there.

Satisfied, he left the office and paused there looking up and down the street. Deciding that Renard could wait for him, talking to Sam, the cantankerous old owner of the mercantile, John walked in opposite direction, toward the saloon.

At a corner of a street, a man lit a cheroot and blew the smoke away. John, who didn't like to smoke, coughed at the acrid smell. He stepped back. The man moved away.

John wiped his tearing eyes with his handkerchief and just when he was ready to walk away too, from the narrow alley between the two buildings a woman dressed in black, with the face partly covered by a veil called him.

"Sir, could you help me please? Oh, I don't

know what to do. I desperately need help," she implored him in an anguished voice. She lifted the veil and a young face with doe-like brown eyes and a hallo of dark curls looked at him. She had a bow shaped pink mouth and an equally pink tip of her tongue moistened her lip, showing her deep anxiety.

She was not exactly beautiful, but she was attractive and vibrant, animated by deep emotion like this, and also very warm and feminine. What man worth his salt could resist such an emotional damsel in distress?

She cried again, "Please," and grabbing his hand pulled him in the alley.

"Of course I'll help you," John said.

She looked around at the deserted place. Then, with a swift movement she raised her hand armed with a long knife she'd kept in the folds of her voluminous skirt and stabbed him. A reflexive gesture made John move his body sideways and the knife struck between his chest and his arm avoiding by an inch to deal a fatal blow to his heart. It had only

scratched his chest, enough to make him grimace with pain.

He didn't know how his knees gave way and he fell to the ground. He felt a rustling of skirts and a vague lavender scent.

"Oh, what have I done? I didn't mean to kill him. I wanted only to wound him," she wailed and after more swishing of skirts, steps running away announced that she was gone.

He felt weak like a kitten and couldn't even keep his eyes open. He didn't know how long time passed until he heard a familiar voice. "Can you get up?"

Never had he been so happy to see his foreman. "Renard, run after her and catch her."

"Catch who? Besides, I can't leave you alone. You bled like a pig. I think whoever used you for target, hit an artery. Let's get you to Dr. Pendergast. His office is not far from here. Here, lean on me." No wonder he felt so lightheaded almost to the point of fainting if he'd lost blood. With some effort – John

was not a tiny man – Renard succeeded to lift him upright and to carry and drag him to the wagon.

"Shall I go to the sheriff?" he asked John, while driving carefully, avoiding jarring him and causing more bleeding.

"No. No sheriff." John didn't know why he opposed involving the sheriff in this and if there was any connection with the attack on Toby, but he felt the mystery of the woman in black was better kept secret for now. It was his to solve.

"You talked about a woman. Was she one of the girls at the saloon?"

"No, she wasn't." It was an effort to talk or to keep his eyes open. "Please, don't tell anyone… Promise."

Renard shook his head. He didn't understand why not to talk. If a woman stabbed his boss intending to kill him, the sheriff should be alerted. Wounded as he was, John Gorman could do nothing for now. "I promise," he muttered. What could he do if his boss wanted this attack on him kept private?

This didn't mean that Renard couldn't try to find the woman himself.

"What do we have here?" the jovial short doctor asked when Renard carried John inside and helped him lay down on the bed. The doctor rolled up his sleeves and washed his hands.

"He stumbled and fell on his knife," Renard improvised, uncaring that the gossipy people in town would think his boss was a fumbling idiot. In fact, Renard was mad at him. A man who let a woman come at him with a knife, distracted maybe by her pretty eyes and not paying attention at her intentions, such man was a fumbling idiot. John was so good at sensing when a man was going to draw on him, but had been unaware when the woman pulled out her knife. Go figure.

The doctor paused and looked at him in disbelief. "Not John Gorman. He's better than that."

"What can I tell you, Doctor? It happens to the best," Renard concluded philosophically.

CHAPTER 11

Dr. Pendergast's wife, who assisted him as his nurse, was a tall, thin woman, with the face marred by a permanent scowl and a dour expression. She shook her finger at John. "Live by the sword, die by the sword," she said emphatically.

"Yes, thank you. I know my Bible," John answered through gritted teeth, trying not to howl in pain while the doctor was stitching his wound.

Finally the doctor stepped back satisfied. "Finest stitches I ever made. Here, I did my best. I cleaned your wound and disinfected it with carbolic acid and stitched it closed. You're lucky your foreman brought you here immediately. If you don't have fever overnight, then it's probable the wound won't turn putrid."

"Could you bind it tightly so I can ride my horse?" John asked him.

The doctor looked at him horrified. "You can't ride a horse, Mr. Gorman. You have to stay in bed several days until the wound heals and then take it easy without any strenuous activity. You lost a lot of blood, don't forget."

"That's impossible, doctor. I have a ranch and it doesn't run itself."

"The wound can get infected. You should stay with us a few days to be sure it's healing properly," the doctor argued.

The loss of blood made John weak. He was aware that he won't go anywhere this evening. "I'll stay here overnight, but I'll go home tomorrow. I have business to attend. Besides you said the wound would heal if I'm not feverish overnight."

The doctor finished putting away his surgical instruments and closed the cabinet. His wife had finished bandaging John, still looking at him sternly.

The doctor, a jovial man with a bald head looked at him smiling. "All right, Mr. Gorman. You rest now. I'll see you later on when I return from the Jacksons. The missus is expecting her seventh child. She was in labor since this morning so I don't think it will be long now."

The doctor left. His wife turned the gas lamp low and went to her business. Renard had left earlier to meet Wayne at the mercantile and to tell him to take Celia home. He said he'd remain in town overnight and he'd be back later to see how John fared.

After looking at the cracks in the white wall in front of the bed, John's eyes closed and he dozed off, exhausted after the ordeal of being stabbed and the pain endured during the doctor's ministrations.

He couldn't say how much time had passed when he was abruptly awakened by the doctor's wife, who turned on the lamp and looked at him disapprovingly. "You have a visitor, Mr. Gorman. Her being dressed in black doesn't fool me. Be aware that we don't allow any lascivious behavior in here. You have ten minutes."

Then she left as abruptly as she had come.

John pushed himself up in a sitting position and tried to make sense of what she'd said. How could she imagine that he was capable of any lascivious doings in his weakened state? First, he thought Celia had come to see him and he cheered up. Then he remembered that the visitor was dressed in black and he feared that it was the mysterious lady who was here to finish him off.

His guess was confirmed when the strong carbolic acid smell from the nurse was replaced by the scent of lavender. The woman entered the room, dressed in black and wearing a hat with a black veil that covered her face.

John touched his belt, remembering that the nurse had removed his holster when he had been brought in. No gun to fight off an attacker. If she wanted to use her knife again, he supposed he could fend her off, even with only one able hand and weak as he was. If she had a gun hidden somewhere in her skirts, then he'd probably meet his Maker sooner than he'd expected. He could cry for help, although he doubted the scowling nurse would come to his aid any time soon.

The woman guessed what he was thinking because she raised both of her palms up in a gesture to show him she was unarmed and meant no harm.

"I wanted to assure myself that you were not dead," she said in a husky voice, unlike her previous cries for help. Those had been part of her acting, of course.

John wondered if this was also a drama enactment and what was the purpose of it. "Why? Why did you stab me? I've never met you in my life. I'm sure or I'd have remembered."

"You killed many people," she said accusingly.

"Not so many. I shot at people who drew on me first, people who attacked my ranch or my friends and neighbors. This is life. A man does what he needs to do in order to survive and protect his own," John replied annoyed.

She stepped closer. "You are a gunslinger and kill for pay. You rob travelers and shoot them."

Now he got really angry. "You're mistaken. I'm a rancher and no one pays me, except when I sell my cattle. Lady, you mistake me for someone else."

She shook her head. "No. I've been told you shot many people, good and bad alike. It makes no difference to you."

"That's not true. Who told you that?"

She hesitated before saying, "The person I trust the most in the world."

Probably her lover, John thought disgusted. Women had a tendency to blindly believe all the lies a man told them, even when he was a bad man, like Esmé's outlaw. He remembered the blind faith beautiful Esmé had in her outlaw.

Women were stubborn creatures. John doubted she would listen to reason and accept his explanation. "And because a man told you so, you decided to kill me," he concluded bitterly. He could be dead now only because the silly woman listened to her lover.

"I didn't mean to kill you. I wanted only to wound your gun arm."

Now that made no sense. "Why did you strike

my left side? It's obvious I shoot with my right hand like most men."

She covered her mouth with her hand over the veil. "Oh, I missed it then, didn't I? I didn't think. My knees were shaking and I was afraid. I failed."

Whoever had manipulated her into stabbing him frightened her. John wondered if she'd been afraid of him or afraid of failing the man who'd pushed her to do it. He tried to find out more. "So why did you do it?" He supposed stabbing a man was not an easy thing to do for a delicate woman, although there were many women throughout history who had no hesitation to kill when it suited them.

This woman didn't seem to be one of them though. "Was it for revenge? Because of a particular man you think I shot or just in general to rid the world of the gunslinger you think I am?"

She kept silent, unmoving, and John thought she would not answer. He didn't pressure her. He'd learned that if you wanted an answer, you had to be patient. When she spoke it was so low that he needed to make an effort to hear. "You killed a person I loved the most. I wanted to disable you for the moment. It was important that you won't be able to shoot… to attack…"

Just when he thought she was going to give him the information he wanted, the nurse opened the door and announced that the time for visit was over.

The woman in black turned around to go.

"Wait," John said. "Mrs. Pendergast, I need a minute more to talk to her. Please be so kind and give us more privacy," he said in a tone that brooked no argument.

It worked and the stern nurse closed the door again.

"Miss… I don't know your name. I'm John Gorman and I have a ranch north of Laramie. I'm well known in town and no one would call me a gunslinger. Ask around."

Mutely she shook her head. Darn, John hated mysteries. "Tell me your name." She shook her head again, more vehemently. "Come on, it's only fair to

know the name of the person who stabbed me. The doctor warned me that if my wound gets putrid I could die," he added.

"Faith," she whispered and opening the door, she ran out.

Did she say, 'have faith' or plain 'Faith' as in her name was Faith. In the end, he found nothing to help him understand what was going on. She thought John had killed a person she loved, and that he was a danger to someone she held dear and she also believed he would attack that person soon. What a muddle!

The nurse entered the room and her pursed lips warned him that he was in trouble.

"Look at you! You're bleeding again, Mr. Gorman. I knew all this agitation was not good for you. I had forbidden the lady to visit you, but she was persistent. If not for her mourning, I wouldn't have let her in."

"In mourning? Hmm." John didn't believe her black clothes to be but a clever disguise. What if she really was in mourning? It was a path to investigate.

"Do you know her?" he asked the doctor's wife.

This gave her pause. "I've seen her in town, I think. I'm not sure who she is. Are you telling me you don't know who visited you?" she asked skeptical.

"This morning was the first time I've ever seen her."

"Then why did she visit you? And why did you receive her?"

"I was hoping she might shed some light on… "

The nurse scoffed. "…on why you fell on your knife," she filled in.

"Yes, possibly. But I found nothing. She just wanted to know if I survived."

The severe nurse shook her bony finger at him and John knew he was going to be served another of her philosophical observations. "Those who play with fire, get burnt."

John's wound started to give him pain and he'd had enough. "I've never played with fire in my life, Mrs. Pendergast. It was all work and work again from morning till night."

She frowned. "I have to check your wound. It's bleeding again. I'm afraid it will need more stitches."

"No more stitches, no way," he grumbled.

The nurse pulled off his bandage and made a tsking sound of disapproval. Then she poured some liquid over the wound that made him yelp at the sudden burning pain.

"Are you trying to kill me, woman?"

"Certainly not, Mr. Gorman. You are doing a pretty good job at this yourself," she replied seriously. Then she dressed the wound again. "There. The stitches were not torn after all," she said, almost with disappointment that she couldn't assist to another round of torture. Then she pulled a cover over him, turned the lamp low, and left the room.

CHAPTER 12

There was no crowd in front of the mercantile. A few years ago, people in town used to come here not only to buy what they needed, but also to socialize and exchange bits of gossip. Now, not so much. They preferred to do their shopping at the Trabing store, opened in 1883 at the corner of Second and Garfield in a large, modern building, well-lit, kept clean and well organized, with several clerks willing to help the customers find what they needed and also what they didn't need, but were tempted to buy.

Call him old fashioned, but Renard liked the old mercantile, dingy and with the counter full of a hodge-podge of merchandise from bolts of fabric and boxes of nails and shoes. It reminded him of the trading posts of his childhood in the Canadian wilderness. He even liked old Sam, the grumpy owner of the mercantile, a man as unwilling to change and accept these modern times as Renard.

He found Wayne inside talking animatedly

with Sam and pointing to a piece of paper laid on top of all the merchandise on the counter. Sam was frowning and shaking his head in disbelief.

"It is the way of the future, mark my words," Wayne concluded, carefully folding the piece of paper and returning it to his pocket.

Sam scoffed and turned to Renard. "Pshaw, a horseless carriage. Do you believe in these crazy things?"

"No, I don't. But I think it's better for our youth to try to build a horseless wagon or a flying machine if they are so inclined, instead of robbing banks or trains."

"Hmm. You might be right. I have your order ready. Do you want me to help you load the wagon?" Sam asked Renard, pressed by a more practical issue.

"Not now. Boss decided to stay in town another day. Could you keep the order until tomorrow?"

"Sure. Whenever you need it," Sam assured him. If he hoped for more details about the change of plan, he was disappointed. Renard thanked him and left the store followed by Wayne.

Outside, Renard stopped on the boardwalk. He took out his pipe as he always did when he needed to think. "You have to take Cousin Celia back to the ranch. And watch out for any signs of danger. We'll return tomorrow if nothing unforeseeable happens," he told Wayne.

"Should I expect danger?" Wayne asked.

"Possibly." Renard came closer. "Boss was attacked and stabbed with a knife. I took him to Doc Pendergast. For reasons of his own, he wants to keep it secret. I believe that it's better to be aware that there is a threat. Be careful. Now I'm going to the boarding house to get a room for the night."

Wayne wrinkled his nose. "That boardinghouse near the saloon is a rough place."

"I'm a rough man. It suits me."

Wayne looked after Renard for a few moments. Yes, after the attack on Toby and now on Gorman, they could expect more to come. They eliminated Toby's killers, but their leader, the one that planned it all, was still at large. He could always hire other killers to do his crimes. Like a snake, if you didn't crush the head, then it would continue to bite.

He walked back to the dressmaker where he'd left Celia. The buggy was stopped in front and a man was casually leaning on its side. His hat was pulled low on his brow, shadowing his face, but Wayne would have known him anywhere. His nemesis. Deputy Sheriff Gabe McCarthy was smiling at him lazily.

"I was wondering how long until you showed up back here?" McCarthy said.

"How did you know I returned to Laramie? Ah, right. Gorman told you," Wayne answered his own question. "And what do you want? Let me guess, you changed your mind and will meet me in the street to see who is the fastest gun," he continued, trying to raise McCarthy's ire.

The deputy was not impressed. "This is my town Dunbar. I have to assure the safety of its citizens, not to create a dangerous conflict. And I have to know if a man is set on doing mischief."

"Aren't you curious which one of us is the fastest draw?"

McCarthy laughed. "Nope. I already know the answer. And so did your reckless father ten years ago when he entered that saloon and challenged me. You'd think he had a death wish. I hope you're not stepping in his shoes." He pointed to the milliner's shop, near the dressmaker. "Gorman's cousin is there. By the way, nice vehicle you're driving today. I like the fringes. And you're lucky. The previous owner, Miss Vanessa Warner, had a string of bells attached to the top." The deputy opened the door at the milliner and ushered Wayne inside.

Celia was talking to a young woman who was arranging a monstrously huge hat on Celia's head. Fake flowers, ribbons, feathers adorned the brim and even a silk bird was perched on one side.

Celia smiled widely when she saw Wayne. "What do you think? Isn't this a wonderful creation?

You can't find something so fancy in the most exclusive boutiques in Philadelphia," she said turning this way and that way to see herself better in the mirror.

"I bet you can't," Wayne muttered.

McCarthy elbowed him discreetly. "Priscilla, as in 'Miss Priscilla's World of Fashion', the proprietor of this shop, is my affianced bride," he announced with pride.

Celia clapped her hands. "How wonderful! Congratulations. When is the wedding going to be?"

"In two weeks," Priscilla answered, looking at the deputy with a warm smile. "John Gorman is invited and I hope you two could come as well."

"Oh, I arrived in town unexpectedly, sort of… I mean, Cousin John had no idea that I'd stop here on my way to San Francisco. So I don't want to interfere with your plans for the wedding."

"Are you kidding? This is Laramie. When there's a wedding, everyone comes to wish the couple the best in life," the milliner answered. "Please come.

The more the merrier."

In the end, Celia settled on a smaller hat with fewer ornaments, that she decided to wear right then. It was very fetching and fit well with her blue outfit. Even Wayne had to admit. "You look pretty Miss Celia."

She blushed shyly, obviously pleased with the compliment.

"Yes, you do indeed," the deputy added his praise, examining a similarly very ornate confection adorning the head of a mannequin. "Do these really sell?" he asked his fiancée with doubt in his voice.

"Of course, they do," she answered swatting his hand away from the cascading purple feathers that erupted like a fountain from the left side of the hat. "I just sold one recently to Cora Lynn Turner, now Mallory. She likes flamboyant clothes and hats that make a statement proclaiming her the queen of town."

"Cora Lynn… Mallory. The one with the piano," Wayne said, remembering the scene at the train depot.

The deputy turned to him. “How do you know about the piano?”

“It’s the talk of town, Gabe,” Priscilla said placing a hand on his arm.

Celia was in a talkative mood. Still admiring her hat in the mirror she started explaining. “We were at the train depot to send a telegram to my Aunt Clara in San Francisco and three drunk ruffians stopped us looking for trouble…” She picked up a light blue flower. “Isn’t this pretty?” she asked Priscilla distracted.

The deputy inclined his head toward the door. “We’ll wait for you outside at the buggy, ma’am.” And he pushed Wayne outside. Once there, he said in firm voice. “Now tell me what happened.”

Wayne bristled at the curt order, but he was going to return to the ranch and he’d have to postpone investigating the mysterious shooter. It made sense to tell the deputy all the details and to let him fret about piecing it all together. After all, it was his job and strangely, Wayne felt he could trust McCarthy. In fact, he even liked the deputy, a man very similar with Wayne himself, born and raised in the west, without a loving family around him. They were both orphans, Wayne growing up without a father and McCarthy raised by a professional gambler, who was not much of a father and who had never bothered to adopt him legally.

So he told him the story about what happened earlier that day at the train station, with all the details he could remember. "Are the three cowboys who work for rancher Mallory connected to the shooter? I don't know. Was the shooter taking advantage of seeing us there or did he plan it all with them? Was I the target and for what reason? Or maybe he mistook me for Gorman because I was driving Miss Celia and the fancy buggy is one of a kind and easily identified. I have no answers to all this and now I have to drive Miss Celia back to the ranch and I can't investigate. I would give anything to be able to search that empty building across the train depot."

"I'll do it. It could be a separate incident, but I doubt it. I think it all goes back to Gorman and his chasing after the outlaws. Maybe even to the man who ordered Toby and his sister murdered. We'll find him," the deputy assured him.

It was on Wayne's tongue to tell him to go see John Gorman at the doctor's and find out more details. The attack on him was probably connected with the shooter at the train depot. He sighed. Renard wanted to keep that a secret and Wayne owed him - if not to Gorman - the loyalty to do as asked.

Celia came out resplendent in her new hat, waved at Priscilla and they were off driving back to the ranch.

"I had a great day," she said happily. Wayne wondered what kind of entertainment she'd had in Philadelphia, if fighting off three drunk cowboys and visiting a dingy garage with a future horseless carriage was her idea of a great day. "Such fancy stores and friendly people," she elaborated, patting the silk flowers on her newly acquired hat. She turned to him. “Wayne, could you show me how to drive the buggy?”

Wayne was scouring the vast expanse of the high prairie for any possible danger or places where attackers laid in wait for the buggy to come closer. He turned to her and looked at her. She was so innocent and unsuspecting. “Now?” he asked.

“Of course, now. What better time than now? We still have at least half an hour before we get to the ranch.”

“I was hoping to be there before dark.”

CHAPTER 13

"Back in Philadelphia, Daddy used to make me take the reins, but in the park there were a lot of other people driving, riding or simply walking, and it was difficult to learn to drive, although I tried a couple of times."

"It seems like your father is a good and open-minded man," Wayne remarked transferring the reins to her.

"Oh, yes, a wonderful man," she agreed dropping the reins and wiping her eyes.

Wayne took the reins again. "Then why did you leave your parents and your home in haste, without money or clothes, and without telling anyone?"

She straightened up and raised her chin, a sign that she was going to dig her heels in and keep her secrets.

"Now, Miss Celia, you asked me about my life and I told you what I told no man. Turnabout is fair.

Tell me. It will help me and Gorman protect you from whatever danger will come your way, if there is someone you're running from."

She fidgeted on the seat, rearranged her hat, and when Wayne thought he was not going to have an answer, she started talking. "My parents died last year in a boating accident. They drowned."

If he'd expected the predictable story of a young girl rebelling against a future marriage arranged by the parents, he couldn't have been more wrong. "Do you suspect anyone caused the accident on purpose?"

"No. Sometimes I wished I had a person to blame for taking my parents away from me. It was just an accident. Or that's what I was told." She was trembling and Wayne regretted pushing her to talk if it was so obviously painful for her. "We were a loving family just the three of us, after my aunt Clara married a banker from San Francisco and moved to the west coast. After my parents' passing, I was overwhelmed with grief and also hurt and confused about what was going to happen to me. I was twenty-two and legally I needed no guardian. As my father's lawyer explained to me, I was the only heir to my parents' estate. My father's man of business, Mr. Mason, assured me that he'd take care of all the financial issues as before. He had been with my father for many years, so I had no reason to doubt him."

"Your trust was misplaced," Wayne guessed.

Celia nodded. "For a while, I signed all the papers he placed in front of me without reading them or giving them much thought. I was still in mourning. Until one day, when I looked at what was written there before I signed. I didn't understand all the legal terms, but it was clear that I was signing all control of the company and my personal fortune over to him. He didn't even pretend that it was not true. He told me that, as a young woman, I had no idea how to run my life, not to mention a large business."

"That's when you ran away?"

"No. I tore up the papers and told him he was fired. He said that it was only a matter of time until the judge will approve his petition to… practically run my life. I went to the bank and, first the teller, then the banker, friend of my father, informed me that without Mr. Mason's approval he can't in all good conscience release my money to me. I was sure to squander it. My monthly allowance set by Mr. Mason was not due yet. I realized I was fighting a losing battle."

"Was there no one to help you?"

She shook her head. "I had no immediate family in town and I was not sure whom to trust from the so-called friends of the family. During the day, I had a cook and a maid with me, but at night, I was alone. One night, two men broke into my house. I heard noises and found them in my father's office searching his desk. I had my father's gun in my nightstand, so when I shot at them and started shouting, they left. It was then that I decided to run away. I packed light only a change of clothes and I took the money that I had, which was enough only for a ticket to Laramie in the Wyoming Territories. I bought it without hesitation. I had to distance myself from the nightmare my life in Philadelphia had become. Maybe I'm not safe here either, but it can't be worse than what it was back East."

"Miss Celia, rest assured that as long as you're with me, you're safe. I promise you that. No harm will come to you. I'll make sure of that," Wayne told her very seriously.

"Thank you. I appreciate it. I'm sorry that your boss assigned you this duty, to drive me around and keep me safe. I know you'd rather be elsewhere," she said.

He didn't rush to deny politely. He knew he would hate to serve as escort to a spoiled rich girl, driving a girly vehicle. But Celia was not a spoiled girl as he had just found out. She was a courageous woman who'd fought the best she could against adversity. He admired her for that. And he discovered that he liked to be with her. Even the pink-fringed buggy suited her and he didn't mind driving it with her. "I don't mind. And now that I know your story, you need someone to protect you all the time. I don't mind being that person, Miss Celia. And John Gorman is not my boss. Renard asked me to help him and I agreed, that's all."

Wayne stopped talking abruptly. There was trouble ahead. Three riders came galloping.

"Indians," Celia cried and grabbed the rifle at her feet.

Wayne rolled his eyes and pushed the rifle down. "This is 1888 Miss Celia. These days, Indians are peaceful and more civilized than some men I know. The older man in the middle is Four Fingers. You've met him. Best healer around."

Reluctantly, Celia placed the rifle back at her feet. "Yes, I did. He loves Cook's biscuits. Always comes down and snatches one from the platter when she isn't looking."

"Four Fingers lives with the Maitlands at Circle M Ranch, although lately he's visited John Gorman's ranch often."

Celia laughed. "For the Cook, or for the

biscuits."

"He has his reasons. He helped Pierce Monroe, the sheriff's younger brother clean the place from Warner and his hirelings. He's well liked by the ranchers in the area. The other two riding with him are his cousins."

The old Indian stopped his horse, looked at Wayne driving the buggy with the pink fringes ruffled by the evening breeze and kept his face stony, although his eyes were alit with amusement. "Where is Gorman and Red Fox?"

"They stayed in town overnight. They'll be back tomorrow."

Four Fingers nodded his understanding. "Trouble?"

"Yeah," Wayne confirmed. "Gorman will explain what kind when he'll be back. I wasn't there. How is Toby?"

"He's young. He'll live."

"Bless you, Four Fingers. His wounds were gruesome. He wouldn't have survived without your

ministrations." Wayne saw that the Indian wanted to say something, but hesitated because of Celia's presence. "What happened? Talk."

But the Indian just made a sign with his hand and the three riders turned around and Wayne started the buggy driving after them. He hoped nothing wrong had happened at the ranch.

After a short distance, they stopped and Four Fingers dismounted. Leaving the other two to stay with Celia, he signaled Wayne to follow him.

After a short hesitation, Wayne jumped down from the buggy. "I'll be back fast. You'll be safe with them."

"Wait," Celia cried after him. "I'm coming with you."

Four Fingers shook his head. Whatever was ahead of them, he didn't want Celia to see it.

"Stay here," Wayne told her firmly and taking his rifle, he ran after the old Indian. Despite his age, Four Fingers was quite fit and fast.

Beyond the rock formation, on top of the knoll,

two men had been shot dead. The first one had been struck in the chest, right when he was talking unsuspecting. His mouth and eyes were open in shocking horror. They found the second one farther away, shot in the back, probably as he was attempting to run away.

"These are the two remaining squatters that Parker kicked off his land. They were a plague, but no one deserves to be shot in the back," Wayne said.

A lugubrious moan made him aware that the man was still breathing, although when he turned him face up, the rattling sounds he made showed that he didn't have long. He was making an effort to say something. Wayne bent to hear him better.

"...demon," was the only word he heard clearly. Then the man rolled his eyes and was gone from this world.

"He was afraid the devil will come to take him. He should have thought of that before starting a life of crime," Wayne said turning away from the dead.

"Maybe," Four Fingers was not convinced

that's what the man wanted to say. "Perhaps he intended to reveal who was the man who shot them."

Wayne shrugged. "We'll never know. I'll send one of the ranch hands to bury them."

"No need. You go on to the ranch. We'll take care of them."

They returned to where they'd left the buggy and Celia breathed deeply, relieved to see him back. Wayne climbed up near her, and taking the reins, signaled the horses to move on. He was in a somber mood and Celia didn't ask him anything, sensing he won't say much. She placed her hand on his arm and with his left hand he patted it, thanking her silently for her understanding.

At the ranch, Mathias approached him with other news. He was a good man, hard-working and honest, but he didn't like to have the responsibility of the whole ranch, especially in murky times with trouble on the horizon. He was happy to see Wayne and to relinquish his duty to him.

"What happened to John?" he asked worried.

Not knowing how much to say, Wayne chose to be evasive. "He decided to stay in town overnight to finish his business. He and Renard will return tomorrow. That's all I know."

Mathis shook his head. "I wish he'd come back today. I sent the boys back to Toby's cabin to clean it up and they found it ransacked. Now, why would someone search that place, I ask you. To steal what? Toby's patched work clothes?" He scratched his bald head and placed his hat back on.

That the person who ordered Toby and his sister shot came back was a surprise. What was he after? And was this the reason they were shot? Did they have anything of value wanted by their killer? – Wayne wondered.

He found Toby much improved, although not entirely recovered. But when Wayne asked him all these questions, Toby had no answer. He only knew that the man who had abused his sister in the past was the only one who had reason to want revenge on her for leaving him and running away. Too bad he

had no idea who this man was.

CHAPTER 14

The sun was setting and it was almost dark. While the rest of the town quieted down, this neighborhood with smaller houses and poor people, with saloons and other less respectable locales, became more circulated and noisy.

Renard walked slowly down the road to Tom Wilkes' saloon. Across the street, a woman accompanied by two men stopped to listen to what one of them was saying, then laughed out loud, stridently. They walked farther and turned around the corner.

The light in the windows of one of the local newspapers was turned off and that side of the street was plunged into darkness. Only the saloon was brightly lit, alive with noise and music.

A man tumbled out of the saloon through the swinging doors and landed in a heap in the middle of the road. He got up with some difficulty and unsteady on his feet, inebriated he made his way to the other side of the street. He stopped in front of Renard, squinted at him, then unhurriedly took out his gun. Frowning he checked it and pointed it at the redheaded giant in front of him.

"You give me your money, mister. Right now. I need to buy me some whiskey and I lost mine. Easy come, easy go," he said hiccupping, in his drunken state ignoring that the man in front of him was double his size.

Renard looked at the drunkard, grabbed the hand with the gun and careful to keep it aimed away from both of them, twisted his arm making him drop the gun with a yelp. "Go and sober up somewhere."

The man rubbed his wrist, and only now seemed to consider the difference between their sizes. He shrugged. "Well, it was worth a try," he muttered and bent to pick up his gun.

"Nope." Renard placed his booted foot on top of the gun. "This stays here. You don't need it."

From a distance, the noise of approaching horses distracted them. Three riders came at fast speed and stopped their hard ridden horses in front of the saloon. They dismounted and tied the animals to the hitching rail. A nervous horse snorted and the rider pulled the bridle tighter.

Renard winced. He hated people who mistreated their animals. The drunkard scurried away.

"The Mallory brothers are back in town," a voice near him commented. It was Jesse, a young orphan boy who survived doing odd jobs at the stables or at the train depot.

"What do you know about them?" Renard asked.

Jesse looked at him and extended his hand palm up. Renard placed a few coins there. The boy nodded satisfied. "The three of them were known rabble-rousers back in the days when their father still lived. It was before my time, but so I heard. The eldest, Duncan married a poor girl when they were both young, and to the old man's disappointment he had only one child, a daughter. Now the daughter is eighteen or twenty, but she doesn't come to town often. Her mother passed away and Duncan remarried immediately Cora Lynn Turner."

Hmm, that was interesting. "What about the other two?"

"Damian and Dan. They do what Duncan asks because he's the eldest, but Damian has a vicious character, cruel to people and animals alike. I think he would stick a knife in Duncan's back without hesitation if it suited his plans."

Renard tossed Jesse another coin. "Now go home, boy. I'll go to the saloon to see what's going on."

"Good luck, mister. If you intend to pick a fight with the Mallorys, you'll need it." And Jesse vanished into the night as silently as he had come.

Due to his imposing figure and red hair, every time Renard entered a new place, he attracted people's stares. This time, when he entered the saloon no one looked his way. They were all more interested in the scene going on at the bar.

The eldest Mallory brother hit the counter with his fist. “Tell me where she is”

A weaker man would have been intimidated, but Tom Wilkes was made of sterner stuff and had faced a lot of threatening men in his life. He had to be tough in order to survive in this business. Nothing and no one could reduce him to a shaking weakling. “As you can see, Mallory, I’m tending bar here and have been all evening. I have no idea of your wife’s whereabouts. Why don’t you boys have a drink and a seat at the poker table?”

The man behind Duncan, a head taller than him, grabbed a glass recently poured for a customer who retreated at a safer distance from the belligerent trio. He emptied the glass in one gulp. Then he raised his arm to throw it at the mirrored wall behind the bar.

Renard approached the bar, not straight from the entrance, but going around the room unobserved. He caught Damian’s wrist and tightened his hold until he dropped the glass. “I’m partial to the mirror

and to the quality of this locale. I don't like to see it destroyed." He looked up and winked at the painting of the naked lady hanging high above the mirror, titled Danae, whoever she might have been.

As soon as he let go of the man's arm, Damian went for his gun. He barely touched his holster, when a loud click froze him on the spot.

"Not so fast, Mallory." Deputy Sheriff Gabe McCarthy had his own gun drawn. "Hands up," he ordered.

Damian Mallory turned to face him, his previous adversary, Renard, now forgotten. His eyes narrowed and the left one was twitching nervously. "You're not the sheriff in this town McCarthy. You can't tell me what to do."

McCarthy pointed at the silver star pinned on his shirt. "This badge says I can. But even without this official authority, I wouldn't let you come in here and destroy Wilkes' saloon."

During this conversation, Tom Wilkes looked at one of the girls and slightly inclined his head

toward the upper floor. She nodded, smiled at the man she was with at the poker table, and moving slowly, she made her way up the stairs, disappearing from sight. After a few moments, she returned near the railings and nodded at Tom.

In front of him, the confrontation between the deputy and the middle Mallory brother continued.

"Why don't we see who is the fastest draw?" Damian said his right arm inching lower toward his gun, hoping to provoke the deputy.

McCarthy shook his head, his gun still pointed at the other man. "No. I'm not going to endanger people's lives and damage Tom Wilkes' property. That's not why I was hired as a deputy sheriff in this town."

"You're a coward," Damian hurled the worst insult at him.

The deputy only smiled. "I don't have to prove my worth or my courage to anyone. Certainly not to you."

"I'll show…," was all Damian got to say, his

hand touching his gun, when his older brother, Duncan slapped him hard over the face spinning him around.

"You idiot, he'll have you shot dead before you knew what happened. He is as good as people say. I saw him in action," Duncan admonished his brother.

Renard stepped back out of the center stage of action. He saw what he needed to know. So that was how the shorter Duncan kept the other two to his order, through sheer willpower.

Just like that, the belligerence went out of Damian. Only the hatred in his eyes promised a retribution for this public humiliation. And this would come when Duncan would least expect, a knife in the back, as Jesse had predicted.

But not yet. Now was not the time to confront his brother. Not in public with so many witnesses. Damian muttered only, "I'm not the one who married that hussy..."

Duncan raised an eyebrow at him. "Watch your language when you talk about Mrs. Mallory.

Now let's go upstairs to see what's going on there."

Renard had seen enough. He left the deputy there, as McCarthy had a firm grip on the situation and was well able to take care of things alone. Unobserved as he'd entered, Renard walked out.

Outside, he looked down the street pondering what to do next. From the alley between the saloon and the next building, a dark shadow turned into the street, hurrying away. It was a woman with her skirts billowing behind her.

"Wait, Miss!" Renard said, hurrying to catch her. It made her increase her pace to escape her pursuer. She was no match for him though. He reached her and caught her arm, turning her around right under a lamppost.

Years of facing both beasts and humans had honed Renard's reflexes finely and he was not caught unaware. He avoided narrowly the strike of her knife. He captured her hand again and took her knife from her. She was hissing like a cornered cat trying to escape.

What were the odds this was John Gorman's mysterious attacker? Dressed in black, roaming the streets and back alleys, handling the knife without hesitation. It could be. Only it was not – Renard was almost sure. John Gorman talked about a young girl and this one was not. The light from the post showed a face that perhaps had been pretty at one time, but now showed marks of a life of dissipation and vice. She surely was not the one John wanted to protect from the law despite being stabbed by her.

"Well, well, Cora Lynn Turner, we meet again."

"It's Mrs. Mallory now," she spat, pulling her hand from his grip and showing that maybe life had altered her youthful beauty, but not her haughtiness.

He nodded amused. "Of course, I know. And so did the people in the saloon tonight. Your... new husband was looking for you and was rather vocal and displeased at not finding you."

She muttered something like, 'the fool'.

"Oh, he might be a fool. But don't forget the

buttered bread comes from him. And if I were you, I'd watch out for his health. You don't want to be dependent on his brother Damian's good will, in case something happens to your husband."

"Ohh!" she huffed her impatience and twirling on her heel she ran away.

Looking after her, Renard shook his head. He wondered if he was wasting his time with the domestic drama in the Mallory family and how – if at all – was this connected to the knife-yielding attacker of his boss.

"That one is no good, hombre." He heard a voice from the shadow of the porch in front of the next door building. A man with his face partly covered by a large sombrero was nodding off on a bench there. "Esta usada."

"Yeah, I know. I mistook her for another woman," Renard told him. He looked at the Mexican considering how much to tell him. He had to ask if he wanted answers, despite John wanting to keep this a secret. The older man could see a lot from his position there and it looked like he knew a lot. It was worth a try. "Maybe you can help me. I am looking for a woman, younger, dressed all in dark clothes and veiled. Have you seen her?"

A flicker of emotion lit the older man's face as he pulled his hat back from his face. Then it was gone. His expression shuttered and Renard could have believed he'd imagined it. "No, I haven't seen her."

"Her life might be in danger," Renard prevaricated in hope of changing his mind and unlocking whatever secrets the man was hiding.

"Could be, but I still can't tell you more," the man finally said, pulling back his large hat over his eyes, sign that he was not talking any longer.

If he had any doubts remaining, they vanished. Renard was convinced the man knew more than he wanted to say. He searched his pocket and pulled out a coin. "Just in case you remember her. I'm Renard and I'll be at the boarding house south of here. If I'm not there, then leave word for me." He threw the coin and the man caught it deftly despite having his eyes

covered by the sombrero and pretending to be asleep.

CHAPTER 15

Early next morning, Renard knocked on the door at the doctor's office. The nurse opened the door and looked at him askance.

"This is not a visiting hour," she said without inviting him in.

"The good doctor is available at any hour when someone is hurt or wounded," Renard replied unfazed and entered the office looking for his boss.

He found John Gorman sitting on the edge of the medical cot and buttoning his shirt. John cheered up when he saw him. "Ah, Renard, help me get out of here."

"How do you feel?"

"As well as expected. But I swear I slept better outdoors, under the stars, on the hard ground, than on this lumpy cot with a spring that was poking my back and with someone snoring so loudly upstairs that it was shaking the house." He got up and smiled satisfied. "I'm good. No more feeling woozy. What about you, my friend?"

"I can't complain. I found out some interesting things about the Mallory brothers. I'm not sure how they fit into all this mystery, except that wherever we go these days we stumble upon them or their men. I found an old man, spending most of his time on a porch close to the saloon. He knows more than he wants to say about everything that goes on in town."

John looked around the room. "The dragon took away my gun."

"Here, she placed it in the drawer." Renard gave it to him and John buckled his holster.

"I have to find the woman," he said.

"The one who stabbed you? I bet you do. I don't know why you want to keep it a secret. Deputy McCarthy could help you find her and put her in jail."

"No, I couldn't. It was a mistake and she was worried about me."

Renard looked at him in disbelief. "Was she? Before or after she tried to kill you?"

"After, of course. She came here to assure herself that I was well."

"She came here? Why? To finish you off?"

John huffed with impatience. "I told you. She thought I was an outlaw who killed without hesitation. And she only wanted to wound me, to disable my gun hand."

Renard shook his head. "Boss, you are one of the toughest men I know and an excellent gunman. But when it's about women you are as green as a young lad. Last year, you were in love with a woman who told you straight that she loves another. And you still dream of her. Get over it. Now, a faithless woman tries to kill you and you believe all the nonsense she is telling you. It is obvious she has an interest and your good health is not it."

Well, put this way, the whole story seemed farfetched, but John remembered the woman's soft brown eyes and felt a warm fuzzy feeling in his heart. She was not lying, he decided. If it was a wrong judgment, no big deal. No one would regret his being stabbed in a back alley. "Let's get out of here," he told Renard.

There was no one in the front office and they left the building closing the door behind them. Outside, Renard inhaled the fresh October air. "I don't like doctor's quarters. They smell of sickness and putrid wounds." He turned around the corner and walked toward the saloon. This early in the day, the saloon was quiet without much activity and the streets around here deserted.

The previous conversation made John curious about his foreman, this almost wild and untamed man. "Tell me, Renard, have you ever been in love?"

"I don't know about love. When I was very young I lived with an Indian woman up north, in Canada," he answered without much emotion in his voice.

"Did you marry her?"

"Nah. I was poor and her father wanted twenty horses for her."

"So, what happened?"

"We ran away south of the Canadian border and lived together for a while. She died in childbirth," he explained matter-of-factly. "No other woman would look at me twice. I'm a drifter. Besides, I don't see myself settling down to raise a family. That's not for me." He stopped short and pointed at a building ahead. "The old man used to sit on that bench and nod off or pretend to. He's not there now."

"Let's see maybe he's inside."

"I don't think he lives here. The building housed a good shoe repair business at one time. It's been abandoned for a while and now it's dilapidated," Renard said carefully approaching the porch and the empty bench.

One of the glass squares in the door was broken. John looked inside. It was abandoned, just as Renard said. He pushed the door open and stepped inside. A table, two chairs and one broken were in the middle of the room. A dirty curtain separated the front space from the back. It fluttered in the breeze created through the open door.

There was nothing here. John turned to go. A slight barely audible swishing sound alerted him of a presence behind the curtain. He pulled it away and the old fabric tore apart. Behind it, the woman in black, without the veil this time, looked at him with eyes full of terror. She raised her hand to her throat to calm her rapid heartbeats.

For a few moments they stood there, unmoving, frozen in place by the shock of the sudden meeting. Then she twirled on her heel and tried to get away.

“Wait! Don’t go,” John told her, grabbing her hand. “Surely you owe me an explanation.”

Mutely, she shook her head and tried again to escape his hold and run away.

The back door popped open and a man with a gun in his hand burst into the house. “Let her go, mister,” he ordered John. The newcomer was young, barely twenty if that old, but the determination with which he pointed the gun proved that he’d shot people before and was not an innocent.

"No, Dan. It's not what you think," she pleaded with him.

It distracted him for a moment, just enough for John to lunge for the gun. He succeeded to make his opponent to drop it to the floor.

The young man went after it. Ignoring the sharp pain in his side, John jumped on the man to stop him from getting the gun.

They rolled on the ground until the man found the foot from the broken chair and hit John. Reflexively, he avoided narrowly to be hit on the head but it struck his shoulder and the pain made him see stars.

Angry now, John punched his adversary in the stomach making him suck in his breath. Not leaving him more time to recover, he clipped him in the chin and the other one fell to the floor cold.

"Good fight," Renard said, extending his hand to help him up. "He is the youngest Mallory brother, Dan. He'll recover. An honest fight never harmed anyone."

John stood up and looked around. The back door was swinging open and the woman had vanished. He pushed it shut frustrated. "Why didn't you go after her?"

"She was not my concern, Boss. You, however, probably popped open the fine stitches the doctor had done with so much care. Now we'll have to go back to have the wound attended again."

"Not in your dreams. The wound will heal eventually. It's only a scratch after all."

"I've seen strong men dying from minor scratches," Renard grumbled. Bending down, he picked up John's hat and slapping it twice on his thigh to remove the dust, he handed it back to John. "Let's go."

"Do you think she was his lover?" John asked, looking from the back door to the man still lying prone on the floor.

"No, I don't," Renard answered curtly, not very happy with his boss' interest in the knife-yielding woman. "If she had even a little affection for him, she'd have stayed to see how the fight ended and to soothe his bruises. She didn't have much interest in him."

"Do you think so?" John asked suddenly cheered.

Outside, on the bench, the old man was back, sleeping unconcerned, with his wide-brimmed hat pulled all over his face, like nothing unusual happened inside the house. It was obvious he was not going to talk and his position invited no more questions.

Very well, he'd keep his secrets – John thought. But Renard was right, the old man knew what was going on and probably knew the woman well.

He turned to him. "Old man, tell her that I'm not an outlaw and never have been. I came from the East two years ago, bought a ranch north of town and have been a rancher ever since. I don't know who told her that I'm a gunslinger, but I've never used my gun except to protect my ranch, my people, and my

neighbors. Life is hard here and a man's gotta do what a man's gotta do."

The hat didn't move, but a low voice said, "There was a rancher called Crawford. His son said you killed him."

"Crawford had attacked my neighbor, Elliott Maitland's ranch. I shot him when he aimed his gun at Maitland's back."

John waited some more, but the hat didn't move and the man kept silent.

"We're wasting our time," Renard said, not only bored, but also annoyed that his boss was trying to justify his actions to the old man, who was not going to change his mind. Stubborn old man!

John was thinking along the same lines, but after a few steps, another idea crossed his mind. He returned to the porch and took out of his pocket the silver coin with the broken chain. He dangled it in front of the old man.

"Have you seen this before?"

The hat fell from the man's face, all pretense

of dozing off forgotten. There was a burning intensity in his eyes and John realized two things. First, that he was not going to get any important information from the old man. He couldn't or wouldn't talk for whatever his reasons. Fear was one of them. And second, that the man was desperate to know more about how the coin had come to be in John's possession. It was there in his eyes, an unspoken pleading. He was dying to know, but even so, he was not going to trade secrets with John.

So be it. Nothing gained, nothing lost. He'd tell him. "One of my men, Toby, lived with his sister and her little boy in a cabin on my land. Last week, three men attacked them and shot them dead." He paused pondering if to tell him that Toby survived, then decided against it. "Renard here is my foreman. He found and buried them. Becky, the woman, had this coin and chain in her hand. I have no idea if it was hers or if she broke it from the neck of one of the killers."

The man nodded, but didn't say anything.

Only two fat tears rolled down on his wrinkled face.

CHAPTER 16

Two horses were tied to the hitching rail outside the saloon. John stepped near the swinging doors and looked over them inside.

"Strangers or some ranchers," Renard concluded after studying the horses.

John signaled him to keep quiet. "Go bring the sheriff," he whispered to Renard.

Inside the saloon, one of the men was holding Tom Wilkes at gunpoint demanding money.

"I make deposits at the bank early every morning," Tom answered looking nervously from one stranger to the other. They caught him dozing in the chair behind the bar or he'd have his own gun in his hand. He'd dealt with the likes of these two drifters all his life. "I don't keep money here from one day to another," he said wondering if he could reach his gun before the man in front saw him.

The second man, a burly miner, had different priorities. He stepped behind the counter and was

examining the bottles lined on the shelves and trying the whiskey content in each one. He wasn't paying attention to Tom, assuming his partner had him covered. He was spreading a pungent smell and Tom wrinkled his nose in distaste. Just then the man took a large swig of malt liquor that was not quite to his taste, so he spewed it out and threw the bottle on the floor.

Looking at the glass shards everywhere, Tom winced. Even if he got out alive today and succeeded to fool them into believing he had no money on him, there would be damage to his saloon. He prayed the large mirror behind the bar would escape unbroken.

"Place all the money and valuables you have on the counter. And better make sure there is enough not to make us mad and my itching finger trigger happy," the one in front of him threatened, waving his gun under Tom's nose suggestively.

His partner threw another bottle on the floor.

Outside, John had seen enough and he decided it was time to intervene. He drew out his gun, pushed

the doors open and walked in.

"Not so fast, mister. Drop your gun," John ordered him.

Instead of complying, the man turned fast and fired a shot that would have killed John if he had not anticipated the move and stepped aside. He hunkered down behind one of the poker tables and shot at his opponent.

The man fell down to the floor dropping his gun and grabbing at his chest. John hadn't shot to kill, but in such a gunfire exchange things were bound to happen. He got up and picked up the man's gun from the floor.

During this, Tom and the other man looked frozen from behind the bar. Not very steady on his feet after all the imbibing, the other robber, drew out his own gun, when a rifle shot resonated in the saloon. The second man fell to the floor crunching the glass pieces spread all over.

John looked up. On top of the stairs, a newer saloon girl scantily clad was leaning her still smoking

rifle on the railing. She looked at Tom to assure herself he was not wounded.

"Thank you, Diana," Tom said nodding at her.

She turned around and disappeared in the hallway at the upper floor as quietly as she had come.

Tom pushed aside the moaning man still lying on the floor and assessed the damage. He'd have to throw away the bottles opened by the robber, but otherwise it was not too bad. It could have been much worse. He turned to thank John.

He chuckled. "I am lucky. You, the man who never darkens my doorstep, are here right when I need help. Thank you." He looked over the counter at the man shot by John. "Is he dead?"

"No, just wounded."

"Same here." Tom pushed again the smelly miner.

The doors swung open and Deputy Sheriff McCarthy entered the saloon, followed by Renard. "What happened here, Tom?" he asked.

"It's like this, Sheriff." Tom called McCarthy

sheriff, even if technically he was only a deputy. That was because Tom respected McCarthy and while Bill Monroe had done a great job as sheriff for fifteen years, now McCarthy did all the work. He deserved the title if he didn't get the pay for being sheriff. "These two men came in with the intention to rob me. One was threatening me with the gun, while the other was destroying my liquor supply."

"I see." McCarthy bent down to look at the two wounded men. "This one figures in a Wanted poster that I remember. Multiple robberies and train attacks." He went behind the bar to look at the drunken one. "I don't know this one," he said pulling his bandanna to cover his nose. "Did you shoot them?"

"Not me. They surprised me nodding off. Not much business at this hour," Tom explained. "I was lucky John Gorman was here and shot them."

McCarthy looked from Tom to John. "Both of them?"

"Yep," Tom confirmed before John could give

more details.

John shrugged. If Tom wanted to keep his saloon girl out of the sheriff's investigation, John had no objection. It didn't matter much who shot the two robbers.

It seemed that the deputy thought the same way, as he accepted the explanation without asking more questions. Of course, McCarthy could see a difference between a gunshot wound and a rifle one. "Renard could you help me lift these two miscreants onto their horses. I'll take them to jail. Doc Pendergast can visit them there."

After the two wounded robbers were removed from the saloon, Tom started to clean the floor, sweeping the glass shards with a broom. "I'd offer you a glass of my prized whiskey if I thought you'd enjoy drinking it."

"Don't waste it on me. I'm not a drinker."

"You and McCarthy both. If all men were like you, I'd be in the poorhouse," Tom said continuing to sweep the floor.

John sensed that the saloonkeeper was still upset and it was not because a few men in town didn't like to drink. "What is it, Tom? Are you upset because they caught you unaware?"

Tom stopped what he was doing, leaned the broom against the wall and came to the bar to face John. He got a bottle with liquor from under the counter and poured some in a small glass. John opened his mouth to say he hadn't changed his mind about having a drink, when the bartender took a large swig from the glass.

"I tell you, Gorman, there is no fool like an old fool." He pointed to himself, nodded and took another gulp of the amber liquid, his prized whiskey – John guessed. "I'm telling you this because you've been here and I know you won't tell anyone. I have no business daydreaming impossible dreams. Not at my age and not in my line of work. It should be all business, nothing more," he confessed sighing and looking furtively upstairs where the girl had been before.

Well, well. The saloonkeeper, the weathered Tom Wilkes was sweet on one of his newly hired girls. Too bad. John didn't think this story could have a happy end. As Tom had said - not in this line of work. But… "Every man needs a nice dream from time to time in order to be able to survive and fight in this hard life. Otherwise, what else is there? Besides, you're not old, Tom. I bet our Sheriff Monroe is older than you and he found happiness after years of chasing outlaws and being alone."

"I'm forty-three. I'm too old for dreaming of happiness. And frankly I was content before, just me and my saloon, watching business prosper." Tom sighed again and placed the bottle back under the counter. "What about you? You're a lonely soul too. Have you ever been in love?"

The image of the beautiful Esmé Richardson, blond and blue-eyed, delicate and sweet, came in front of John's eyes like if she were real. "Sure I was. Every man needs to make a fool of himself at least once in life."

"True," the saloon owner agreed. "Was this back in Philadelphia? Is this why you ran out west?"

"No. It was right here."

Tom frowned. Since John Gorman moved here and bought the Millers' ranch, he was not known to be involved in a love affair. So, who could be the mysterious woman? John did not come to town often. He visited only with his neighbors. What young woman… ? Understanding downed like thunder strike. "Oh man, don't tell me you loved Richardson's sister?" One look at John's face and he had his confirmation. "They said she took her own life after the bounty hunter killed her outlaw lover."

"No, it's not true," John protested, although he didn't know what the truth was. "The family said she went to live with her aunt in Chicago. She was too delicate for life on the ranch."

Tom bent closer. "Women are not as delicate as we like to believe. Of course the family claimed she went away. They don't like to admit if there is any truth in her involvement with the outlaw."

"She went away. Renard confirmed it. Where? Now that is a mystery. So you see, my friend, every man has his own weakness. Don't blame yourself too hard." He must be hit in the head, John thought. Who'd have believed that he'd exchange sappy stories with the saloon owner like the lowest drunkard? Tom liked to gossip, but John was sure that today's conversation would reach no one's ears. Time to get to serious issues. He took out of his pocket the silver coin on the broken chain. "I came to ask you if you remember seeing this."

Tom wiped the counter and squinted at the coin. "I can't say that I've seen it. It's Mexican and most probably belonging to a man. The chain is too thick to be worn by a woman. It could be like a pocket watch chain, if not for the coin. Where did you say you found it?"

"One of my men was attacked. He and his sister and her little boy were shot to death. I don't know why. They were very poor, so robbery was not a reason. The woman had this clutched in her hand.

I'm trying to find out why this senseless crime against innocent people happened."

"Did you find the killers?"

"Yes, I did. They were hired to do this. I'm looking for the person who ordered this crime. I'll find him and make him pay."

Tom nodded. He understood John's motivation to find the man guilty of ordering the cold murder of people he knew, even if Tom personally couldn't help. Honestly, he couldn't remember ever seeing the coin. He would have liked to help John. "I'll ask around. Discreetly," he mentioned.

And with this John had to be content. He left the saloon thinking. Not much progress done this day, other than helping place two robbers behind bars.

After he left, the saloon girl who shot the robber came downstairs, this time dressed in a plain dark skirt and white shirt. "I've seen that necklace with the silver coin before."

Tom looked at her surprised. She came closer and whispered something in his ear. Tom's eyes widened. He shook his head. “I’m not going to send Gorman into that vipers’ nest.”

CHAPTER 17

"Before going home we have to go to the mercantile to load the wagon with whatever Cook wrote on her list," Renard said.

"Hmm, yeah," John agreed, although he'd like to stay a few more days in town to find answers to all the questions he had. Who was the woman dressed in black and who was the person who ordered Toby shot? While these two issues were apparently separate, John's instinct told him they were inter-connected. He needed to find the truth. "You take the wagon and Cook's supplies and go home. I have to stay a day or two in town."

Renard lifted his old-fashioned fur hat and ruffled his red hair like he always did when being uncertain what to do. "I can't leave you here alone and wounded, Boss. I'll stay with you. You need me in case the woman you're after decides to stab you again."

John was not used to his men refusing to do his

bidding. But Renard was stubborn and had a mind of his own and didn't much care about orders. "Be reasonable, Cook needs the supplies and Mathias doesn't like to be in charge of the entire ranch for so long."

"Cook is a very practical Indian woman. If we don't get back, she'll send another ranch hand to get the wagon with supplies and she'll send us our horses. As for Mathias, it's true he's good to organize work on the ranch, but he shies away from too much responsibility. Here comes in Wayne, who is great at taking care of things while we're away."

John stopped right there on the boardwalk. The idea of leaving the gunfighter in charge of his ranch didn't sit well with him. "No way am I going to let that drifter to be responsible for my ranch, the people and animals."

"You might not agree, but I bet it is already a done deal. Mathis has shifted the responsibility onto Wayne and he is the right man to do it. Not to mention he has an incentive to do it right."

"What incentive?" John asked wondering if Renard had taken it upon himself to promise Wayne more money.

"Why, the sweet, pretty Cousin Celia, or have you forgotten about her?" Renard smiled in his red beard.

"If he dares to…" It irked John to no end that Wayne Dunbar was not only in charge of the ranch, but also around the pretty Celia.

"No, I don't mean anything impolite, just old-fashioned courtship. Perfectly acceptable. What did you expect? She is pleasing to the eye and if you choose to run after a knife-stabbing wench, Wayne has to do the polite thing around Miss Celia. You can't run after two rabbits, Boss, and expect to catch both. You have to choose one."

Whatever Renard had to say was interrupted when across the street a man stepped out of a building in a huff, pulling the door shut after him with more force than necessary, rattling it from the hinges. He mounted the horse that had been hitched to the rail in front and beat him hard on the flank with his whip. The animal rolled its eyes in terror and galloped away at high speed.

"I hate men who use whips on horses or other animals," John said looking after the departing rider.

"That was the middle Mallory brother, Damian. You met the youngest, Dan, this morning. I don't know if Damian is the most dangerous of the three, but he's fast to anger and ready to draw."

John looked at the firm sign above the entrance, Melville C. Brown, Attorney-At-Law. "These Mallory brothers turn up at every step I take in town these days. I wonder what he wanted from the lawyer." He pushed the door open and entered the office.

Renard shrugged and followed him. He didn't have high hopes they'd find out anything of use from the attorney. Lawyers were not known to share information easily with strangers about their cases.

Melville C. Brown, the famous attorney was an average looking guy, middle aged, and no one would believe that he could be a real fighter and defend his clients with both shrewdness and vigor. He looked at them above his spectacles. “What can I do for you, gentlemen?”

“My name is John Gorman and I own a ranch north of town.”

The lawyer leaned back in his chair, amused. “Yes, I know you, Mr. Gorman. What kind of lawyer would I be if I didn’t know everyone and everything that’s going on in town? Are you two in need of legal advice?”

“Not exactly. I saw one of the Mallory brothers coming out of your office and I was wondering why he was so angry?”

“I can’t tell you, Mr. Gorman. Attorney-client confidence and all that.” He stopped shuffling papers on his overly-crowded desk and looked at John. “May I ask why you are interested in Mr. Mallory’s affairs?”

“It’s a justified question,” John conceded. “Three people on my ranch were shot to death. I need to find out who ordered this crime. That's why I'm here in town instead of minding my own business and my ranch."

"Do you have reason to believe Mallory committed this crime? Do you have any proof?"

"No, I don't. It's just that no matter where I turn I stumble onto a Mallory brother. Is there a connection? I don't know yet, but I'm persistent. I'll find out and confront the guilty person," John said frustrated to face another dead end.

"I see. As I said, I can't reveal any of my client's business. And I'm sorry that Mr. Mallory left in a state of anger. This is usually the case when a son disagrees with the terms of his father's will," he said crossing his arms over his chest. "I'm sorry I couldn't help you, Mr. Gorman. Come back when you'll be in need of a lawyer."

And with this, John said Good bye and left the office.

"He's a very shrewd man," Renard observed when they were back in the street. "He gave us only

this much to understand Mallory was upset by a family problem that has no connection with any crime."

"Yes. It looks like the middle brother was angry that his father left the ranch to the older one."

"Rumor has it that Damian wouldn't hesitate to kill anyone that stands in his way including his brother."

Outside the dressmaker's shop, Emily Richardson, the owner called him from the door. "Mr. Gorman, I'm so glad to see you. One of the dresses ordered is ready. You can take it with you."

John looked at her dumbfounded. "Dresses? What dresses?"

The smile froze on the face of the nice dressmaker, who was also married to John's neighbor, Lloyd Richardson. "The dresses ordered by your cousin. She said you were paying for them."

Renard elbowed him. "The dresses for Cousin Celia."

"Ah, yes. Those dresses, of course. I'll write

you a check for them. Right now I have business in town for a few days and I can't take them. But I'm sure Celia will come soon to take them. Thank you for helping her." The smile and two dimples appeared again on her face. She was truly a nice, gentle woman. "And how is your family? Any news from your sister-in-law, Esmé?" he asked casually like making polite chit-chat and not having a real interest in the subject.

The dressmaker looked at him with understanding and even compassion. "No, Mr. Gorman, I have no news from her. She's not planning to visit us anytime soon. We keep her in our hearts and prayers and we know she's happy there, where she is. We have to be content with that, accept her choices, and continue with our own lives."

"Very good advice, Mrs. Richardson," Renard interfered. "We'll do the same... Well, sooner or later."

She clapped her hands. "Good. Then let's talk about happier events. Your Cousin Celia, who is a lovely lady, very friendly, she already accepted the invitation to the wedding. I'm sure you got one too."

"What wedding?" John asked wondering if somehow the town had continued to live and move forward, while he was left behind. Social events had never been his forte.

"Really, Mr. Gorman," she admonished him. "The wedding between our Deputy Sheriff Gabe McCarthy and Miss Priscilla from the milliner's shop. Many people plan to attend. They want to convince McCarthy to stay on as Sheriff, considering that Bill Monroe is semi-retired."

"Yes, ma'am. I'll think about it."

"What's there to think about? If your cousin is coming accompanied by that nice man Wayne Dunbar, then you ought to come too." She smiled confident that she had convinced him and turned her attention to Renard. "And you Mr. Renard, if you need a new shirt for the event and for going to church, then you should come to me. I can fit you better than the Trabing store and I'll give you a better price."

Renard, who had never worn anything other than his fringed western leather shirts over his longjohns, nodded meekly. "Yes, ma'am."

A sharp whistle announced the arrival of the afternoon train at the train station. John and Renard walked the short distance to the station along the 1st Street. The passengers were descending on the platform, many of them reunited with relatives and friends waiting for them.

Timmy, the young assistant of the station master was smiling happily. "After all this time working here and I still look in awe at the technical marvel that is the locomotive. A great invention, this is the way of the future."

A man happy with his lot in life, John thought. Good for him. He was looking at the newly arrived passengers and was ready to ask Timmy if he had seen anything unusual, when his eyes stopped on a tall man wearing a dark duster and carrying a portmanteau. He was like any other western travelers, nothing to attract attention. Yet there was a

certain dark aura around him that made John give him a second look.

The man looked around and his nose twitched in displeasure, although the train station was like any other and Laramie was a typical western town, maybe better than others, considering it was a railroad stop.

The newcomer observed Timmy's uniform and walked closer. "Tell me, boy, where could I find a horse for temporary use?"

Although a young man, Timmy was not used to be called 'boy' and in such a derisive way. He raised his chin and answered politely, but curtly. "There are horses for rent at Marty Roberts' Stables in town."

Usually people were friendly and helpful in Laramie like in any other western town, but they expected to be treated with politeness in return. Timmy had two horses and the buggy for this exact purpose, to loan to strangers in need. But he decided to let the arrogant newcomer deal with Marty, who was more interested in his own profit than helping

others.

A gust of wind raised the stranger's duster revealing a neatly buckled holster with two guns on both sides. He narrowed his eyes, but didn't try to pull back the duster to cover his guns. "How far to ride from town to the Mallory ranch?" he asked.

"About half hour riding west of town," Timmy answered, ready to go back to his office.

He left John and Renard there, looking after the stranger walking to the end of the street toward Marty Roberts Stables.

"He's changed, but I'd know him anywhere," Renard said. "Bill Longley, a bounty hunter who crossed the line one time too many and killed twenty-seven people, all in the name of justice. I suppose now he's plainly a gunslinger for hire. Why do you think he's visiting Mallory?"

"Good question. And which one of the Mallorys hired him?"

CHAPTER 18

Celia knocked on the door and entered the room. For several days now, she was bringing breakfast to Toby and spending some time with him. The young man was recovering well and was often sitting in a rocking chair near the window looking outside. As Four Fingers said, he'd survive this ordeal and his body was mending well. His heart was still wounded and mourning his sister and little nephew.

Celia understood his deep grief and after she confessed that she'd suffered a similar loss a year ago, Toby opened up, talking about his loved ones, how much he missed them and the shock of the unexpected attack. He often cried and Celia was compassionate and she knew that he needed to grieve and that he wouldn't do it in the presence of the other ranch hands, being ashamed to show his weakness.

"I've never had a home, Miss Celia. Not the shack where we lived as children with our drunkard father. It's no wonder, Becky ran away Lord knows where and after that I hired here. When she came to me, desperate and with her little boy, John Gorman offered to let us live in the cabin on his land. Becky cleaned it and for the first time in my life I felt the warmth of a home and making a family with my sister and her kid. The attackers took that away from me, because I could never return to live at the cabin where Becky and Josiah were murdered." He sniffed and turned his head away, embarrassed by his tears.

"You have the memories, Toby. And the knowledge that you gave your sister help when she needed it most."

He turned anguished eyes to her. "I failed to protect her. I let her be shot and killed and I don't have the name of the man who ordered us shot. It eats at me that I have to stay here like a weak coward instead of going after the killers."

"Cousin John caught one and transported him to the sheriff. He's now in jail. The others were shot when they ambushed John and his men. So you see, justice was done."

"Not by me. I will not rest easy, not until I find the man who fathered Becky's child. The man who wanted her dead."

If Toby had no idea who this man was, then it was a slim chance to find him. Celia thought that the young man would better go on with his life, remember his sister with love, and forget about more revenge on a ghost he had no chance finding or fighting. But men were like that, set on revenge, and nothing could deter them from this path. Look at Cousin John, instead of returning to the ranch with them, he'd decided to stay a few more days in town. Celia was sure he was pursuing this revenge too. She was worried for his safety.

"Do you miss your home in Philadelphia, Miss Celia?" Toby asked her, willing to change the subject that consumed his every moment, tormenting him.

"No, Toby, I don't. When my parents passed away, the house of so many happy childhood memories ceased to be a home for me." It was a place where she languished from room to room all day, but instead of her parents' loving presence, she met only emptiness and regret for what could had been if her parents were still alive. "Like you, I'm never going back there. I'll make a new life for myself in California. For now, despite what happened to you, I feel safer living here with Cousin John than alone in Philadelphia."

It was the truth. She felt close to this man she'd met only days ago in the train and it came easy on her tongue to call him cousin, even if they were not related by blood. Perhaps she felt like a kinship of sorts because both of them were from Philadelphia.

"Are you going to marry him?" Toby asked, waking her from her daydreaming.

Celia blinked surprised. "Who? Cousin John? No, of course not." She was not even considering marrying John, although she was past the age when the girls got engaged and married. John was very handsome, tall, blond, and blue-eyed, and confident about his lot in life. She liked him very much, but only in a cousinly way. No sense messing their comfortable relationship with other stuff.

Toby smiled. “No, not him. I may be wounded and isolated in here, but I have a good view… “ He pointed to the front yard and all the going-ons out there. “…and good hearing. I was asking about the new man who was driving you all day yesterday.”

Understanding dawned on her. “Wayne? No, of course not,” she repeated primly. “I just met him. I don’t know him.”

“Life is short. We don’t need a long time. When it’s right, we know immediately,” he observed sagely for one so young and not married himself.

“Yes, well, this is not the case,” Celia answered. Confused, she tried to change the subject. She grabbed the book on the table near Toby. “Let me read you from this book.” It was the old Bible that John had brought Toby from the cabin. A good thing he did, because the cabin had been ransacked after that, and while it was doubtful the thieves were interested in religious reading material, old as it was, the Bible would have been destroyed by rough handling. It was barely keeping the pages together in the partly torn cover.

Toby nodded. "Yes, thank you. I would like that. It brings me some temporary peace."

She opened the old Bible and some pages fell on the floor. "Oh, I'm sorry, Toby." She kneeled to pick up all the pages and to place them back in their right order within the cover. One folded piece of paper was newer than the Bible pages. It had been kept inside the Bible.

Carefully, Celia unfolded it and saw that it was a birth certificate. Here in the west, not many people were recording the births of their children officially. In this case, it had been recorded at the office of the Albany county clerk and it had also a proof of baptism from the Episcopalian church for Josiah McDonald, natural son of Duncan Mallory and Rebecca McDonald, born on June 9th, 1886. That was two years previously.

Wordlessly, Celia handed the paper over to Toby.

"I knew it," he exploded. "The old goat was coming to visit her when she was barely sixteen and he a married man." He clenched his fists.

"Toby, you don't have to let grief darken your mind. Maybe he's not the one guilty of your sister's death. After all, a father doesn't order his son killed. It doesn't make sense," Celia tried to reason with him.

"For revenge. Because after years of abuse, she ran away taking the boy with her. You don't know these Mallory people. They are evil."

Celia stood up and pushed the chair to the side. "Toby, you stay here and let your wounds heal. I promise I'll tell Cousin John and I assure you he'll do what is best in order to discover who is the guilty man and to bring him to justice.

"I should be the one to punish him," Toby protested.

"Trust John to do what's right," Celia replied and with this she left the room and went in search of Wayne.

Since both John and Renard were away, all men had turned to Wayne for guidance as what to do, including Mathias. Wayne had stepped in and assumed the task of running the ranch. He was a born leader, Celia admitted.

She found him in the barn, ready to saddle his horse to ride out on the range in search of a calf that one of the men said was mired in a creek.

"Wayne, I need to go to town to talk to Cousin John," she told him agitated.

"Now?" he asked shifting the weight of the saddle. Like any man who had a definite mission in mind, getting off this track was disturbing. "I'm busy now. We have to find the lost calf."

"If you find a man to harness the horse to the buggy I can drive myself to town."

Visions of Celia driving alone and attacked by outlaws or getting lost and becoming prey to wild animals crossed his mind and made him angry. "There is no way you're going alone to town. It's already afternoon and you could get lost in the dark.

Get such an idiotic idea out of your mind."

"It's not idiotic at all," she protested. "Emily Richardson is driving her buggy almost every day. Women do drive alone if they live far from town. I'm not incapable of doing it."

He tightened the cinches to his saddle. It was maddening that she was so stubborn and he couldn't make her see reason. "No," he said making a cutting motion with his hand. "No, and that's final."

In that moment, Celia heard the same words said by the horrid man who'd tried to take over her family business, her finances and practically her entire life. She shook her head. Never again would she let another overbearing man do this to her and dictate what she could or couldn't do.

She narrowed her eyes. "You don't get to say what I can or cannot do. Who do you think you are?"

Wayne stiffened. "That's right. I'm a nobody. The bastard son of a laundress. But I am also the man your cousin charged with your safety. And I take my job seriously, no matter what you think of me." With this he vaulted in the saddle and rode out of the barn.

The minute she said the words, Celia knew she'd made a mistake. In the short time she'd spent with him, she'd realized Wayne Dunbar was a good man, hard, but reliable, honest and proud. Whatever his origins might be, they didn't matter. He was who he was.

"He was only trying to keep you safe, missy," she heard behind her. Mathias pulled the bridle of another saddled horse, preparing to ride out. "He didn't deserve them harsh words. Boss is relying on him to assure your safety and he is doing just that. A good man, that's what he is." Then, he rode out too.

When the men returned, Wayne was not among them.

"Where is he, Mathias?" Celia asked.

The old ranch hand looked at her with understanding. "He's out there, chasing some of his inner demons. He'll be back, don't worry."

But she did worry. Wrapping a blanket around herself, she sat back in the rocking chair and settled down to wait for him.

It was dark when he returned. He took his horse to the barn and when he walked to the front porch he saw her there, rocking slowly.

"I'm sorry," she said simply. "I didn't mean to speak to you disparagingly. I appreciate you very much and I like you. You don't have to take every word spoken in the heat of a dispute as an insult. It was not meant that way."

He sat down on the top step of the porch. He looked tired like he carried the weight of the world on his shoulders. "I had time to think about this too. These are nice words, Miss Celia, but no matter what you say, the truth is you don't think of me as your equal, or consider me like the fine dandies that courted you in the East."

This got her attention and all her plans to behave meekly and make peace went out the door. "Of course I think of you as equal. What a thing to say."

"You wouldn't consider, let's say, marrying

the likes of me," he replied bitterly.

She opened her mouth to talk, then snapped it shut thinking. Finally, she looked at him and said, "You are so immersed in your own perception of inequality that you don't consider others' plight. I would marry any man who would agree to write my own fortune over to me. To give me the freedom to decide what I want and to admit that I have a brain that works and I'm responsible. I would marry this man, who would trust me and give me this right legally. I would marry him right away. Presuming that I like him," she amended.

Slowly, a smile bloomed on his usually stern face. "Good," was all he said.

CHAPTER 19

Same evening, when the street lamps started to be turned on, the newcomer entered Tom Wilkes' saloon. He had been assured that this was the best in town and he needed a stiff drink after the lousy day he'd had today.

He'd been jostled for hours on the wood bench in the train carriage by two portly persons, who had no business traveling, speaking loudly and inconveniencing the other travelers. Then, the stable master told him that he had no available horse to rent to him until next morning when Rancher O'Leary's wife would return the one she needed to carry her supplies home. After telling him more than he wanted to know about the said rancher's wife's many ailments, Marty Roberts, the owner of the stables offered him a donkey, slow, but sure to take him to his destination, the Mallory ranch. Unless, of course, the donkey didn't have one of his stubbornness fits. Then it was anyone's guess when he'd arrive at the

ranch.

That was unacceptable. In his line of work, it was crucial to make an appropriate impression. When he walked by, people should shake with fear and scurry away from his path. It was part of what made him so good and famous. It made his heart pump faster with excitement to chase his quarry and see the panic in his eyes like a rabbit caught in a trap and having no way to escape. What kind of grand impression was he going to project, parading through town and arriving at the ranch riding a donkey? About its stubbornness streak, he wasn't worried. A good whipping was going to make any animal move, and fast.

So, all things considered, he'd decided to stay in town for a night and ride to meet his employers the next day.

He surveyed the saloon with critical eyes. Not bad, he decided. Cleaner than most, enough activity at the poker tables, with girls younger and prettier than he'd seen at other saloons and a lively piano

player.

Satisfied, he walked to the counter. "Whiskey," he ordered curtly.

The bartender poured a glass and pushed it toward him, without asking any questions. Good, the newcomer was annoyed when people were too talkative and nosy. When he raised his eyes, he saw that the bartender was not cowered by his threatening stance. His face shuttered, the bartender went to serve the next customer. For some reason, this displeased the gunfighter. Didn't they feel that a famous person had landed amidst this crowd?

He raised the glass and was cheered by the deep amber color of the liquor. At least, the bartender had the good sense to serve him good whiskey, not watered down. He turned to look at the poker tables. If there was another thing that made his blood boil with excitement apart from chasing a prey and fighting an adversary in a shoot-out, it was gambling at the poker table.

At one of the tables, a young cowboy stood up,

checked his empty pockets and walked away. Unhurriedly, the gunfighter came by and without asking permission, took the empty seat. He placed a cheroot in his mouth and snapped his fingers at the girl who was hovering nearby. She struck a match and lighted his cheroot without trying to flirt with him as her kind was taught to do. Her lack of even pretend eagerness to serve him grated his nerves. Maybe she was young and properly cowered by his imposing figure.

"Leave the bottle here," he told her curtly when she tried to refill his glass. Again, she complied without saying anything.

Soon, he was deeply involved in the game. He was winning heavily, when the person in front of him, a stern, unsmiling rancher announced he was done for the night. The gunfighter didn't like having the game, his fun and winning streak interrupted and thought to force him to stay and put up his land or whatever other values the rancher had.

Before he could do that, the place at the table

was taken by a dandy, newly arrived in town. Unlike the rancher, the dandy was very talkative. This would have annoyed the gunfighter very much if the dandy was asking unwelcome questions. He didn't. He was content to just talk about everything from the weather to the unpleasantness of traveling by any means, from stagecoach to train. He seemed confused or plain brainless, forgetting what cards he discarded and asking to take them back, which was unheard of and unacceptable in the world of poker playing.

The gunfighter suffered no fools and usually he would have chased the dandy away, but the colorfully dressed little man placed on the table a good amount of money and no player at the table would refuse him the chance to loose it all.

So the game went on. And indeed the dandy lost it in a very good natured way, most of it ending in front of the gunfighter. The dandy placed some more coins on the table.

The gunfighter felt warm and a familiar rush through his veins like when he anticipated an important moment would follow. He looked at his hand. Two jacks and two nines. He grabbed his glass only to see it was empty and so was the bottle. Did the others fill their glasses from his bottle? It didn't matter.

"Bring another one," he ordered the girl behind him, throwing the empty bottle to the floor.

He smiled sardonically. Now was his moment. Two pairs with a good chance for a full house was a great hand. But he was a gambler above all, a risk taker. The fifth card was a ten of spade. One of the jacks and one of the nines were also spades. He kept the three spades and discarded the other two.

Slowly he unfurled the two new cards he'd been given. A three of spade and… a nine of diamond. In the end he had nothing much, a pair of nines. Keeping his disappointment inside and his face impassible, he considered folding. He had a large amount of money in front of him. A wave of recklessness swept over him. He pushed all the money in the middle. "I'm all in."

The dandy shook his head, looking at his own hand. He twitched his nose and reluctantly pushed his own money to the center. "Oh, well. Let's see what you have."

The gunfighter blinked, awakened from the dream of a big winning to the stark reality. He'd lost everything he had before and what he'd won this night. How could the dandy know he had no winning hand? His eyes fell on the girl who was now pouring a drink to the man on his right. Anger darkened his sight and his mind. He threw his cards on the table and stood up suddenly sending his chair crushing behind him. "You," he said accusingly. "You signaled him what cards I had." He slapped her hard over the face, making her spin around and fall to the floor.

"She didn't signal me anything. She didn't have to," the dandy protested, showing his own modest hand of two queens. "It was clear to me you were bluffing. The confidence of having won too much and having luck on your side went to your head. I've seen it happen before."

Tom Wilkes came out from behind his bar, the rifle in his hand. “Mister, no one is allowed to treat my girls roughly. I keep a clean business here. You are not welcome any longer. Move along out of my saloon. And I don’t want to see you here again.” He helped the girl up and gently touched her bruised face.

The gunfighter clenched his fists in rage. He turned to leave, but it was not in his character to abandon a fight under threat. He turned again and drew his gun out, firing at Tom’s back, before any of the other customers could react in any way.

“Nobody tells me to leave,” he said looking at Tom’s body lying on the floor face down with a crimson spot on his right shoulder. He twirled his gun around his index finger and with an expert move placed it back in his holster.

He considered taking all the money on the table. He won it, it was rightfully his. The dandy was surely in the cahoots with the girl. He should be glad he was not shot too for cheating.

The girl stepped closer to him, hatred in her eyes. “You killed Tom. Like a coward you shot him in the back.”

She was very close to him now and he raised his hand to slap her again. Some women don’t know their place. They need to be taught.

He didn’t get to do it though. She raised her hand with a Derringer that she had hidden in the pocket of her dress and aimed it straight at his heart. From such a small distance it was impossible to miss.

When the shot came, the gunfighter looked at her incredulous. “You shot me,” he said clutching his chest, before rolling back his eyes and falling to the floor dead.

The customers looked stunned at this rapid development. A moan from Tom made them jump into action. They lifted Tom and helped him sit in a chair. He assessed the situation, then he grimaced in pain and looked at the girl who remained where she was like a statue. “Diana, go upstairs. It will be all right.”

Wordless she climbed the stairs slowly, not looking back.

Tom took a deep breath. "I'll need you folks to help me get to Doc Pendergast. The bullet in my shoulder hurts and it needs to come out. But before, I want to say something. I like to think I keep a clean establishment here. The whiskey is not watered, the place is clean, the piano player is… better than the one before him and my girls are not helping poker players cheat. I shot the man who threatened my customers and my employees. Is that clear? I shot him. If anyone of you present here says otherwise, he'll not be welcome in my saloon ever again. Just remember this well. I shot him," he repeated and paused to take deep breaths. He was afraid he was going to faint before taking care of the business. "Dora," he called a woman who'd been working for him for a long time. "You're in charge until I'm back from the doctor."

With these last words, Tom fainted and slumped in the chair. Two tall men lifted him up and took him outside.

"There, bring him to my wagon," another said, wishing to be helpful.

Tom Wilkes was a strong character and despite his line of business which kept decent ladies away and made him not accepted at the social events, he was liked and respected by men and accepted in church where he donated money periodically.

Dora removed the feathered ornament from her hair and tied Tom's apron over her fancy red dress. "Boys, let's remove this body," she said pointing at the gunfighter's body. "Get him to the undertaker."

"Do you think he's dead?" one of the customers asked.

"Of course," the piano player answered taking his place on the stool in front of the piano. "The girl… I mean, Tom shot him from very close." He started to play a lively tune.

The night was still a way to go and business had to continue uninterrupted. Dora called a girl

from the kitchen to clean the floor and soon there was no trace of the drama that had happened before.

Satisfied, Dora took her place behind the counter. Tonight she was tending bar and if the customers didn't cut her some slack, she was not against using the rifle to scare them away. She didn't have the stomach to shoot a man like the new girl did. Although when a body was pushed, there were no guarantees what a body could do in order to survive.

CHAPTER 20

After spending a night at the boardinghouse close to the train tracks, John felt itching all over. A visit to the barber was in order. He had a relaxing bath and he had his hair trimmed and his face clean shaven. His wound was almost healed and he asked the barber to bandage it again with clean cloth.

Feeling much better, he left Renard at the barber ignoring his protests and went to a newly opened café to have breakfast. It was owned by a middle aged German couple and it was spotlessly clean and served hearty meals.

He was sipping his coffee, somewhat milky for his taste, but good, when he saw Wayne walking fast outside on the boardwalk. John knocked in the window to get his attention and signaled him to come inside.

Wayne sat down at his table and after placing his hat on the chair nearby, bit in one of the pieces of apple strudel on John's plate.

John frowned. "What are you doing in town? I thought you were at the ranch helping Mathias."

"I was. And for the record, Mathias was helping me. Just so we are clear." He finished his strudel piece and looked again at the plate. "Good pastry." John pulled it in front of him, to save the last pieces from Wayne's voracious appetite. Bertha, the owner who was passing by, smiled pleased at Wayne and placed another full plate in front of him. He returned the smile and Bertha pinched his cheek in a motherly fashion before returning to her kitchen.

"Talk," John ordered.

"Miss Celia found out who is the father of Becky's child. Duncan Mallory. It was written on a birth certificate from the office of the county clerk. It looked like Becky wanted his birth recorded officially. It mattered to her to do it. She considered this important. Not many parents bother to record their children's birth. He was also baptized so there must be a record of this at the church. She hid the papers in the old Bible that you found in the cabin and brought it back to Toby. A good thing you did because the cabin was ransacked after you left."

"Mallory again. Wherever I turn these days, facts point to him and there is a connection. Was he the one who ordered his own child killed?"

Wayne nodded. "Toby seems to believe so."

"Hmm. I've seen gunslingers and even outlaws, who wouldn't hesitate to shoot and kill any man who opposed them. But they draw a line at deliberately killing a woman or an innocent child," John replied, not yet convinced. On the contrary, he felt that instead of solving the mystery, the reality became more blurred and he got farther from the truth.

Wayne cleared his throat. "There is more. Unrelated to this, though. Miss Celia wanted to come to town."

"Now? I hope you didn't allow her…"

"Could you not allow her to do whatever she sets her mind to?"

John sighed. "Right. I see your point. She is

rather willful. I pity the poor man who will be so besotted that he'll consider marrying her." Just then Wayne chocked on a morsel of pastry and John slapped him on the back to help dislodge it. "I suppose she is at the dressmaker now."

"We've been there and she was happy with her dresses and other doodads that women absolutely must have. But Mrs. Richardson was not there, only her assistant was, so we left sooner than if the women had some gossip to impart," Wayne explained looking at the bottom of his empty cup.

"I hope you didn't bring her to the boardinghouse."

"I should know better than that," Wayne protested offended. "She wanted to go to church, so I left her with the pastor's wife, who has seven children. Miss Celia pitched right in to help feeding and dressing them."

John scratched his head. "To church? Whatever for? It's not even Sunday."

Their conversation halted when a strong smell

of violets or other flowers assaulted their nostrils making John sneeze. Renard took a seat at their table.

"Have the violets bloomed in October?" John asked, admiring his foreman freshly cleaned, with his hair and beard trimmed.

"Before I could see what he was doing, the barber doused me in cologne. I told him I'll strangle him, naturally. But he was not impressed and said I smell better now."

Wayne nodded. "He was right, although he could have shown some restraint. I bet he made you pay for the whole bottle of cologne."

"Oh, he wanted to, but I was so mad that he agreed that it was for free."

"He should have offered another bath also, to get rid of most of this smell," John mumbled wiping his watery eyes.

From the front of the store, they heard Bertha shouting. "You little thief. You stole the strudel. I'll whip your behind if I catch you again."

"I ain't stolen nothing," a young boy protested.

"I have business with Mr. Gorman there."

Renard stood up and walked up front. He threw some money on the counter. "For your effort and whatever loss, Mrs. Kanner. And pack some pastry for me and several pieces of that good strudel of yours. I'll take care of this young lad."

He placed a hand on the boy's shoulder and ushered him to the table. The boy, Jesse, took a seat and voiced his protest. "I ain't stolen nothing," he repeated sullenly. "And if I did, she'd never had known or caught me. I know how to make things disappear without being seen."

He brightened up at the sight of food and started to wolf it down. Renard waited patiently for him to finish and packed back in the paper the leftovers. He handed them to the boy. "Now tell us what business that is so fiery up important you have with Mr. Gorman."

"Ah, yes," Jesse said ignoring the napkin and wiping his mouth with his not so clean sleeve. "Mr. Gorman, the old Mexican man from near the saloon wants to see you now. He said it's important."

"Why didn't you say that sooner," John said, placing his hat on and raising to go.

Renard shook his head and grabbed the boy's skinny wrist. "If you're sending us to a trap, boy, remember I can find you even if you hide in a rat's hole."

"No, mister. There's no trap," Jesse denied. "The old man is sick and dying and he wanted to talk to the tall, blond rancher, he said. I'll take you there."

The three men followed the boy down the street, past two of the saloons, to the not so good area of town until they reached the abandoned house with a bench in front near the entrance where the old man used to spend the day watching the passers-by. Now the bench was empty and the whole place was lugubrious and silent.

Jesse turned to face them. "I'll take only the rancher Gorman. That's what the old man said. You two can wait here."

"Why is that, boy?" Wayne asked. "The whole

thing is fishy, if you ask me."

But John didn't feel any threat and he thought that it was possible the old man wanted to communicate an important fact or message to him alone. "Wait here. I'll go with the boy. You'll hear if a fight starts inside."

Neither Renard, nor Wayne was happy with his decision, but they had no choice and waited outside.

Inside, the place looked as before with the dusty table and the broken chair nearby. Jesse walked passed the torn curtain into the kitchen. John followed him, but the room was empty. There was no one there. Maybe Wayne had been right. The whole place was creepy.

"Does the old man live here?" he asked the boy.

"Not here, but close," the boy answered and opened the back door, going outside behind the house. There was a tiny dwelling, more like a shack than a house and Jesse pushed the door open.

John had to bend down to get inside. Cautiously, he looked around waiting for his eyes to adapt from light to the darkness inside. He saw a cot near the wall, where the old man was laying with his eyes closed. Only his raspy breathing showed that he was still alive.

"What's wrong with him?" John asked Jesse. "He was fine two days ago."

Jesse shrugged. "When you're old, it just happens. You know when the time to go has come," he concluded with surprising insight for someone so young. "Now, I have to go. You'll be fine with him. There is no trap." And he opened the door again and walked away, leaving John alone with the old man.

John approached the bed and looked at the wrinkled face that laid still. Sensing he was being watched, the old man opened his eyes.

"Thank you for coming. Do you still have the silver coin and the chain?" he asked unexpectedly.

John took it out of his pocket. He hesitated to part with the only thing connected to Becky and possibly the man who ordered the killing. He hadn't solved the mystery yet. But then he shrugged. It didn't matter. Toby had not claimed it as a family object. He handed it to the old man who clutched it in his hand with surprising vigor for one so feeble.

"It's mine," the old man whispered. "I was there, in Veracruz in 1858 with Juarez. Ah, what glorious times! I kept this as a memory, and later, I gave it to my daughter."

It didn't make sense. Was the old man's mind completely lost that he didn't know what he was talking about? "Who is your daughter?"

"Was," the old man wailed. "She was the wife of Duncan Mallory and she died last year. She was killed by robbers who attacked their carriage when they returned home. Or so I was told."

"I'm sorry for your loss. If she's dead, then how can I help you? And how did the silver coin get to be in the hands of Toby's sister? Another woman shot dead. And what is the connection?" He was fumbling in the dark and nowhere close to the truth.

“You can help me.” The old man grabbed John’s hand. His eyes were feverish. “You said you knew my granddaughter was in danger. Help protect her. It’s all I want before passing on into the world of the shadows. I want to make sure, my little Isabel is safe. Promise me to protect her, to keep her safe.”

“Who is she?” Isabel. The mysterious woman dressed in black and covered by a veil. It made sense.

“Isabel Mallory, daughter of Duncan Mallory. My own daughter is dead, but I need to know Isabel is going to be safe.”

CHAPTER 21

The door opened and the beautiful girl came in. Now she had a name, Isabel. It suited her, John thought, ignoring that her eyes were flashing daggers at him.

"You, what are you doing here with Grandpa?" she asked him.

The old man raised his eyes at her. "Isabel, be reasonable. I called him. He's a good man and you need his protection. Besides, he brought your Mama's silver coin back to me. Isn't that a miracle? A sign from above that everything comes full circle and he is the one meant for you?"

"Grandpa, do you have fever again? Why do you think he has Mama's coin? Ask him?" she pleaded with her grandfather.

"I know why. He told me."

"Did he? I bet he told you his lies. Papa told me what happened. He was the robber who attacked them when they returned home from town, a year ago. In the fight Mama was fatally shot." She turned to John. "You killed my mother," she cried. Her fists were clenched and she looked at him with smoldering angry dark eyes.

"What? I never shot a woman in my life." He took a step back shocked by the staggering accusation.

"Yes, you did. Papa told me how you attacked them. And my father never lies to me." She took the coin and the broken chain from the old man and raised it in front of John's face. "How else could you get this necklace if not from my mother?"

"My foreman found it clutched in the hand of a woman who lived in a cabin on my land. Her brother, her little boy and herself had been killed by hired gunmen. Why? I have yet to discover."

She shook her head in denial. "No, no. Why would a strange woman have Mama's necklace?"

"That's another thing I aim to find out. Why was Becky McDonald holding that coin like a way to point us to the man who ordered them murdered?"

"Probably they were attacked by robbers," she said. "Why else?"

"Not really. Nothing was stolen and they were very poor people. There was nothing there to steal."

"You invented this entire story. Who's to say it's true?"

"While she and her child are dead, her brother, Toby survived his wounds and he's recovering at my ranch. He can and will confirm what happened in front of a judge. And make no mistake, I will have no peace until I find out the truth and bring the man guilty of their death to justice."

"Grandpa, you don't believe this, do you?" she asked, grasping at straws to hold on to the reality that made sense to her and the truth her father told her.

Before the old man answered, John talked again. "I don't know what your father told you, but I'm a rancher. I have never attacked or robbed anyone. I'm an honorable man. I'm sorry about your mother, but I had no part in that attack and I have no idea why your father blamed me of all people."

The old man nodded in agreement. “Listen to him, girl. He’s a good man.”

“Why do you believe him?”

“Because I asked people in town, many and diverse people. They all confirmed what I already knew, that he is an honest, hard-working rancher.”

She seemed to hesitate for a moment, then hardened her look on John. “How about rancher Crawford? Do you deny you killed him?”

“Certainly not. Crawford and his hirelings were attacking my neighbor, Elliott Maitland. I caught him trying to shoot Maitland in the back in his barn. I shot him without hesitation. There are rules in a man’s world and one of them is that only the lowest coward would shoot a man in the back instead of confronting him face-to-face,” John replied annoyed to have to explain his actions to this girl, who probably was not going to believe him anyhow.

“Gorman here, also refused the challenge by Crawford’s son. He knew that in a shoot-out he was going to have to kill him.” The old man nodded.

"That's the kind of man he is. It happened at the saloon and I was there. Isabel, you need to get away from the Mallory ranch. That place is not safe for you any longer."

"What are you talking about, Grandpa? The ranch is my home. Of course I'm safe there. Papa loves me," she argued.

The old man sighed. "Maybe he did before. People change. He's changed. He lied to you about how your mother died. And since he married that vicious woman, you're not safe there any longer. Please let John Gorman take care of you. He wants to keep you safe and he's the only one able to confront the Mallorys. You need a strong man and he is that."

She looked at him confused. "Cora Lynn is not so bad. Papa was alone and she's been a comfort to him."

"Don't be naïve, girl. That woman gambles at night upstairs at Tom Wilkes' saloon. She cheated on banker Turner until he divorced her. It's common knowledge in town."

"She said Turner was abusive."

"You live isolated there at the ranch, but she's bad news and what's more, your father knew this before he married her. She probably blackmailed him. She knew a secret about him that could have been damaging. So he married her. This is the reality."

"Oh, I want life to be as it was before Mama died."

"I want that too, girl. But it's not going to happen. I'll see her soon in heaven. Until then, I want to make sure you are safe. Go with Gorman."

She looked at John and sniffed like a small child. "How can I leave my home and go with him when there are so many unanswered questions. "How did Mama die? And why was her necklace in the hand of a strange woman? It doesn't make sense."

John closed his eyes for a second. What he was about to tell her would shake her world even more and he would have gladly spared her if he could. But it was time she knew the truth. For too long her father had kept her in a cocoon of lies and she was now in danger because of this. "There is more, Isabel. My cousin has found in Toby's old Bible a proof of birth recorded at the county clerk office. There was also a proof of baptism, so I assume there are church records too. Toby's sister was unmarried and her little boy was fatherless. He was two years old. The name recorded as father of the boy is Duncan Mallory.

She looked at him in horror. "No. It can't be. If he was two years old, then it means my father knew his mother at least three years ago when Mama was still alive. No, this can't be true. I don't believe it."

"Believe it, Isabel," her grandfather said. "Mallory visited the saloon often and… other places. It's true that in his mind he didn't attach much importance to this. It was his due as a man and your mother was forced to pretend she didn't know."

"But if you knew, why didn't you tell me?"

"It was not my place to tell. And I didn't know about the little boy."

She was shaking like a leaf in the wind and John extended a hand to comfort her, to absorb part of the shock of having her whole world upside-down. She ignored it and suddenly turned on her heel.

"I have to ask him what is true and what not. It can't be all bad." With this, she ran out the door.

John wanted to follow her immediately, but the old man stopped him. "Let her go. She needs to confront her father and find out the truth for herself. In an hour or two will be dark. Then you go to the Mallory ranch and take her with you. I'm afraid the truth will come out with the force of an explosive. Be there to take care of my Isabel. Promise me."

John didn't hesitate. "I promise."

The old man closed his eyes and fell back on his pillow exhausted.

Outside, Renard was sitting on the bench waiting for him.

"Where is Wayne?"

"He went to bring three horses. He anticipated we'll need them," Renard explained looking at John amused. "The girl came out huffing and puffing, so I assume a drama took place in there."

"Yeah. She found out her father she loved is a cheating liar. Not exactly a pleasant surprise," John added taking a seat near his foreman. "We wait for Wayne here. I hope he is not coming with three old nags from Marty Roberts' stables. They'll expire at the end of the street."

"No. Cook sent a man to retrieve her wagon with supplies. He brought us our own horses."

"That's better. We have to ride in the dark to the Mallory ranch."

Renard rubbed his hands with glee. "Finally, some action. It was becoming boring dealing only with old men and women into drama. I have some news."

"Good or bad," John asked bracing for what was to come.

"Of both kinds. Do you remember the slick gunman who arrived yesterday with the midday train? He stopped at the saloon to have a drink and play some cards. He picked a fight and shot Tom Wilkes in the back. Tom killed him."

"After being shot in the back?"

Renard nodded. "That's the story. Of course someone told me in confidence that it might have been one of the younger girls who did it."

"And he's dead?"

"Yep. He's at the undertaker."

"What about Tom? Is he all right? He's quite a character in this town."

""Yes, he's fine. Doc Pendergast took his bullet out and now he's back at the saloon unlike the gunslinger who's dead."

"Was this the good or bad news?"

"The good. The bad news is that the two saloon robbers – remember them? – broke out of jail and took the man we brought in, Toby's attacker, with them."

John slapped his thigh with his hat. "How did they escape?"

"Jeremiah was in the Sheriff's Office, how

else? They conked him in the head and opened the cells."

"This happens one time too many."

"True. But McCarthy can't be in two places in the same time. And of course our sheriff is in a prolonged honeymoon."

"Some people are lucky, don't be envious. We need to hire a new deputy."

"Bah," Renard scoffed. "We need a solid lock on the jail and to take the keys away from Jeremiah."

CHAPTER 22

The ranch was nestled in a valley at the foot of a hill. When they saw the ranch lights in the distance they slowed down and finally stopped their horses behind an outcrop of rocks.

"Renard, you stay here to guard the horses. Without them we're like rabbits in a trap. We have nowhere to run or hide," John said dismounting. "Wayne, you come with me. While I'll try to see what's going on inside the house, you stay behind me and watch around us for any unexpected person that might discover our presence there."

Covered by darkness, they approached the house cautiously. A skittish mare was tied to a post near the front door. Wayne touched her gently and gave her a sugar cube. She blew in his palm in appreciation. Wayne signaled to John that he could climb the steps to the front porch. Then he took his gun out of his holster and looked around.

The barn doors were open. Not a good sign.

Either some ranch hand had been careless or there was someone inside. And the mare showed signs that she'd been ridden recently. Was someone visiting the Mallorys? Not the outlaws recently escaped from the Sheriff's jail. The mare was too well groomed and cared for to belong to them.

The front door opened suddenly and Wayne barely had time to hide in the darkness, one with the wall. The man who came outside didn't pay attention to his surroundings. He lit a cheroot and walked to the barn with an unsteady gait.

Wayne shook his head. Was there no limit to these people's carelessness? If an ember from the cigar fell on the dry hay, the whole barn could go up in flames.

After sticking to the wall not to be seen, John looked inside through the large window from what was the parlor. The window was covered by a thin gauzy curtain, which allowed him to see inside, but the people inside couldn't see him in the darkness of the night. The window was not locked so he pushed it an inch open.

There were only three persons in the room. Duncan Mallory was standing near the fireplace, leaning against the mantel, looking thunderous. Cora Lynn was sitting poker straight on a Victorian settee and Isabel was pacing the room agitated.

"…and the man you hired didn't show up," Mallory addressed Cora Lynn with reproach in his voice.

"That's because he got himself involved in a fight at the saloon and got himself killed," she answered calmly.

Mallory whistled. "He was supposed to be one of the best. Who shot him?"

"Tom Wilkes. But I think there is more to this story. Who knows what the truth is." She pursed her lips in dissatisfaction. "I don't like it when the prey becomes predator and people die closer to us than I'd be comfortable."

Isabel stopped her pacing and turned to her father. "Papa, forget the newly hired man. You'll hire another. I asked you to tell me the truth about how Mama died."

Mallory waved his hand impatient. "I told you. The robbers who attacked us shot her. What more do you want? I bet that stupid old man flapped his mouth more than he should."

"Leave my grandpa alone. What really happened to Mama?" she asked with tears in her eyes.

Cora Lynn narrowed her eyes. "Maybe she should know the truth. You spoiled her and protected her too much. She's an adult and she should know life is not a fairy tale. It's hard and often ugly. And the truth hurts."

"Papa, what happened?"

Mallory looked at her aggravated, but he started to talk. "We were coming home and Damian chose that moment to pick a fight with me. You know your uncle. Always ready to argue and contradict me. In a fit of anger, he pulled out his gun and fired at me. Your Mama got in the way, and unfortunately, she was fatally wounded. It was an accident."

"Uncle Damian killed my mother," Isabel pronounced slowly, trying to perceive this truth, contradicting what she'd believed until now.

"I told you. He didn't mean to. You know how he is, high-tempered and quick to anger."

"No, he meant to kill you, not her. Does it make this better? And you try to hide it, instead of making him pay for such a crime."

"He's family, Isabel. If he goes to prison for murder, the entire family suffers by association."

"So instead, you fabricated the story about being attacked by robbers and accused an innocent man of this crime."

"You pestered me all the time to tell you more. I didn't report him to the sheriff, did I?"

"No, because the whole town knew the truth. John Gorman is an honest rancher, a respectable man. Why did you tell me it was him?"

Mallory looked at her sheepishly. "He was new in town at the time and people said he was fast with a gun. He'd just shot and killed Crawford. He could have been a hired gunslinger. And better accuse him, then reveal it was your uncle Damian."

"Stop protecting your brother, Papa. He should pay for killing Mama. And who ordered the murder of the other woman?"

"What other woman?" Mallory asked genuinely surprised.

"The one that had my mother's coin necklace." She took out of her pocket the broken chain and raised it up. "This one. Why was Mama's necklace in possession of this woman who was shot by paid killers?"

Several emotions crossed Mallory's face, first understanding, then regret. He closed his eyes for a moment to recover from the surprise. When he opened them, he was back in control. "It doesn't matter any longer. She's dead."

"No more lies, Papa. She had a two year old boy and you were his father. I had a little brother and I didn't know. How could you?"

"I didn't know. She left before telling me she was expecting my child. She just vanished."

"Probably because she wanted to raise her son in peace, but she was not allowed. Who killed her?"

"That's enough, girl," Cora Lynn said in a very authoritative voice, standing up. "Stop hounding your father. He was not involved in the killing of this woman and even if he was, it doesn't matter now. She was a nobody."

"She was a woman with a child who was my brother. How can you be so insensitive, Cora Lynn?" Isabel wiped her eyes. "You can be, can't you? I found out that you are not exactly lily-white, either. You gamble at the saloon upstairs and you cheated on poor banker Turner. That's why he divorced you."

"Shut up or I'll make you. Stop spreading lies about me." Cora Lynn yelled at Isabel enraged.

"I'm not spreading any lies. The whole town knows this apparently. Papa, why did you marry her? You knew. You must have known what she is."

A malicious smile spread on Cora Lynn's face.

"Because I had proof that your dear Papa had killed a man in cold blood. It was a long time ago, but he could still go to prison or even be hanged for it. So you see, girl, before talking trash about me, look at your own family first."

"That's enough, Cora Lynn," Mallory told her sternly.

"Is this true, Papa?"

He covered his forehead briefly with his hand, in an attempt to chase away the past. "I was young and impetuous, like your Uncle Damian is now. Fights occurred often between men and let's not forget that the whole territory was much more wild and rowdy then. Not much law enforcement."

"Live and learn, young lady," Cora Lynn said with the same superior smile on her face. "And stop talking nonsense about me or else. Don't forget I have the upper hand."

Yes, the gloves were off, Isabel thought. No more pretending to be the nice stepmother. A wave of rebellion went through her. That vicious woman had no right to tell her what to do. "I don't fear you. The people in town know you well enough. You can pretend to be a grand lady, but folks know better. You're the same as the girls at the saloon. Worse. They had no choice, you did."

Cora Lynn's face was mottled red with anger. "You stupid girl, don't you dare talk to me like that. I'll show you." Fury darkened her mind. She took out of her pocket a small gun and fired at Isabel.

At the same time, her father stepped in front of her. The bullet hit him squarely in the chest. He fell down.

"Papa," Isabel cried, kneeling on the floor near him, supporting his head.

"Go… away from… here. Far away… Love…" And with this his head turned to the left and slid from her hands. Duncan Mallory exhaled his last breath.

"You killed him," Isabel said in disbelief raising her eyes to Cora Lynn.

An unholy gleam was in her stepmother's eyes.

She raised her gun again and pointed at Isabel. "And now it's your turn." She pulled the trigger, but either the gun was stuck or it had only one bullet and it didn't work.

Cora Lynn looked at the gun, frowned and then tried again. Nothing.

Isabel sprang up and ran out the door. Outside, she jumped in the saddle of the mare and rode away fast, frightened by all that happened to her today.

From the barn, a man ran out and fired his rifle in her direction. He was far off mark and Wayne shot him before he tried again.

"We've seen and heard enough. Let's get out of here," John told him and they vanished into the darkness.

Renard was waiting for them near the horses.

"Mallory is dead," John told him mounting up. "Where is Isabel?"

"She rode ahead like the hounds of hell were after her. I bet she's going to the old man. We'll catch her soon. Her mare is feisty like her, but she's no match for our horses." Saying this, Renard turned his horse and they rode away after the girl.

At a turn in the road, they were stopped by a volley of fire.

"Isabel, stop shooting. It's us. Come out," John shouted at her.

The young woman came from behind a boulder, pulling the mare along. The fight had gone out of her and she looked exhausted.

John dismounted. "Come here," he told her and opened his arms. With a small cry, she ran to him and hid her face in his shirt. He touched her dark hair and smoothed it gently.

"I want to go to grandpa," she said raising her eyes to him, like a child who needed to find the only anchor that she still had in her life, so tormented recently.

CHAPTER 23

Despite the late hour, the old man was waiting outside the house in his usual place on the bench. As soon as Isabel saw him, she slid from the saddle and ran to him.

"Oh, Grandpa, Papa is dead. Cora Lynn shot him," she wailed distressed.

Lovingly he stroked her hair. "I'm sorry, Isabel. I know you loved him and in his own way, tormented as he was, he loved you."

She raised her head and looked at him, her eyes brimming with tears. "She wanted to shoot me and he stepped in front of me. He saved my life."

The old man nodded. "He did the right thing. He brought your mother a lot of anguish, but in the end he redeemed himself. The Lord will forgive him."

"Uncle Damian shot Mama by mistake. And we still don't know why her necklace was in the hand of that woman. So many unanswered questions and now we're not going to find the truth."

John stepped on the porch. "Isabel, take your grandfather inside. Renard and Wayne will wait for me here and will make sure nothing happens to you."

"Where are you going?" she asked.

"To pay a visit and get some answers."

Wayne looked at him askance. "A visit at this hour? It's close to midnight."

"Exactly. It's the right hour to get answers from stubborn people," John answered cryptically. "What about you? Don't you have to see what happened to Cousin Celia?"

"No. I arranged for her to sleep in the pastor's loft. Snug as a bug."

"Snug is the right word. How will the pastor, his wife and their seven children accommodate a guest in their already tight lodgings?"

"For a night they'll be fine, all of them in one room and Celia in the loft. I paid the pastor a good amount of money. They are a proud bunch and don't accept charity or even help. People give him money for the church, forgetting that he is in need too.

They'll be fine."

"Very well then. Keep an eye on Isabel while I'm gone. I won't be long." Saying this John walked away. Not far. He made it to the right and two blocks down the street he stopped in front of a townhouse. 'Melville C. Brown, Attorney-At-Law' said the firm above the entrance and there was a light in the room at the second floor.

The door was locked and John banged the doorknocker several times making enough noise to alert the dogs in the neighborhood.

The window upstairs opened and the famous lawyer dressed in a ruffled nightgown and a night bonnet bent out. "Why are you making such a noise? Ah, John Gorman, did you kill someone and need a good defense lawyer?"

"Not, yet. Now let me in. I need to talk to you."

"It's almost midnight. Can't you come at a more decent hour?" the lawyer grumbled.

"It's important. Besides, your light was on, so I knew you were awake." The lawyer had a big house in town, but often he preferred to work late into the night and slept at his office.

The window was closed and steps sounded on the stairs. Soon the door was opened and the lawyer ushered him in. Carrying a gas lantern in his hand and dressed in the white nightgown he looked like a ghoulish character from a Halloween story.

"Let's go upstairs. It's warmer."

The lawyer led him to a cozy room, with a cot in one corner and the walls covered with shelves with books and a large desk in the middle. "This is my kingdom. At home, my family reigns, here is my place," he said dressing with a comfy-looking plush robe over his nightgown. Then he poured two glasses with amber liquor and took a seat in his chair.

"Now then, tell me what was so fiery important that it couldn't wait until tomorrow."

John looked at him and although he rarely drank alcohol, he took a sip. It burned his throat, but it warmed him up. "Duncan Mallory is dead," he said straight without introduction. "Cora Lynn shot him."

A thought crossed his mind. "She might want to accuse Isabel of the crime, but there are witnesses. I was watching at the window and so was my man, Wayne Dunbar. If it will come to that. I wouldn't put it past that sneaky woman."

"That's why you're here?" the lawyer asked placing his spectacles on and searching among the papers on the desk.

"No. This occurred to me right now. I'm here because I want answers. Isabel needs protection and I still don't know how and why the killing of people living on my land is connected to the Mallorys. I need to understand and right now I'm only grasping at straws. I want straight answers."

The lawyer raised an eyebrow and looked at John speculatively. "Are you the girl's fiancé? In that case, considering the father is dead, I could talk to you.

Darn the lawyers and their convoluted rules and decisions. Life was so much simpler and straightforward. Why couldn't he answer the questions? John thought. Well, if this was what it took, so be it. "Yes, I'm the girl's fiancé."

"If you are, then I don't have good news for you. The old man Mallory, her paternal grandfather left her nothing in his will. Nada, zilch."

"Oh." John breathed easier. He'd been braced for worse news. "But why?" he asked curious. "Isabel is a sweet girl."

"But she is only a girl. Mallory Senior was upset and disappointed by all three of his sons and he wanted a reliable man to take care of his ranch," the lawyer explained.

"So all his sons have been disinherited?"

"That's right. A bitter pill for them to swallow when I informed them of the content of their father's will. And, trust me, it is airtight and can't be contested. I should know. I wrote it."

John frowned in confusion. "The old man Mallory passed away a year or more away. Where was the heir and why didn't he come forward? The Mallory brothers are still living at the ranch."

The lawyer ignored the question and looked at John above his glasses. “Listen, I’m telling you this in confidence because being responsible for the girl, Isabel, you’re entitled to know why she was not mentioned in the will.” He sighed. “I warned the old man that he’s opening a can of worms, but did he listen? No, at this age people are stubborn and set in their decisions.”

John waved his hand impatient. “So, what did he decide?”

“He left his ranch, lock, stock and barrel, his fortune as much as it is, to his first born male grandson, regardless if he was legitimate or not. In this case to the child Josiah McDonald.”

John was stunned by the news. “If you knew this, why didn’t you say anything? They were probably killed for this reason.”

The lawyer inclined his head. “Probably. In fact I contacted the boy’s mother, Becky McDonald, as soon as the old man passed away. She was frightened and wanted nothing to do with the ranch.

She didn't decline the inheritance. But for the moment she was aware that she couldn't fight the Mallory brothers. She was afraid for her son."

"And in the end she couldn't protect him," John observed sadly. The lawyer nodded in agreement and sipped his drink. For a long moment they kept silent, thinking at the fate of poor Becky and her son. "So, if the little boy is dead, what happens to the ranch? Does it revert back to the brothers? It would be so unfair."

The lawyer cleared his throat. "This is the interesting part. In order to protect the little boy, Mallory Senior wrote a provision in his will. If the boy doesn't reach the majority, then the ranch goes to the closest male relative of the boy on his mother's side."

John's jaw dropped in surprise. "This is Toby. Are you telling me that Toby McDonald is the owner of the Mallory ranch and everything that goes with it?"

"That's correct. And that is as far as it goes.

There are no other living relatives of the McDonalds. I think that's why they were all killed."

A slow smile lit John's face. "They were wrong. Toby is alive and recovering from the wounds."

"Really? You said they were all dead."

"I said the hired men were paid to shoot to kill them. My foreman, Renard, found them and brought Toby to the ranch house where an old Indian, Four Fingers patched him up. He is recovering now. Slowly, but he'll live."

"A miracle indeed. Well then, from legal point of view the Mallory ranch belongs to Toby McDonald. Practically, it's another matter. Good luck to Toby to force out the three… two remaining Mallory brothers in order to take possession of the property. I doubt they'd give it up without a fight."

Encouraged by the news and ready to go, John fell back in the chair. "You're right. I didn't think of this. Toby is a soft-spoken, good lad. He's not a ruthless fighter. Not like the Mallorys."

"People toughen up when life demands it. His family was killed. Toby will find unexpected strength to fight. He'll see this like you do, as justice for them, and he'll face it bravely. There's nothing else to do and he has nothing more to lose."

John stood up and extended his hand to the lawyer. "Thank you for telling me all this and helping me make light in this murky business."

Back at the house with porch he found not only his men, Renard and Wayne, Isabel and her grandfather, but also Deputy Gabe McCarthy in deep conversation. One would think it was middle of the day, not well past midnight.

"Gorman, I just told them that we caught the outlaw that you brought us and who escaped yesterday. We shot him in the leg and he was crying like a baby. He broke down and told us that Damian Mallory paid them to have Toby McDonald and his sister killed. Who knows what twisted sort of revenge he had in mind?" the deputy explained.

"I found out why," John told him and explained what the provisions in Mallory's will were.

McCarthy shook his head in wonder while the others commented surprised. "Well, greed is a powerful motivation. It was a night of surprises. Tomorrow I'll gather a posse to go after Damian Mallory for his many crimes. Killing his sister-in-law a year ago, ordering the killing of Toby and his family and more recently, tonight he stabbed a girl at the saloon who refused to serve him more to drink." He saluted and left to continue his nightly rounds before retiring for the night.

Isabel didn't want to leave her grandfather alone in town and she declared she couldn't leave with a man she didn't know, unless her grandfather came with her. The old man signaled John that he wanted to talk to him.

They went to the small house in the back, where the old man, not at all on the brink of expiring, but full of renewed energy, searched under the mattress and brought to light a package with money.

He handed them to John.

"You are an honest man, Gorman. I knew Mallory left nothing to Isabel. Here are five thousand dollars. Enough for a man to buy a good sized ranch. I want you to know Isabel is not a poor girl. This is her dowry. I want you to place it in the bank in her name. I'd be happy if the two of you would get married, but I know these things can't be ordered. Love is or isn't. I rely on you to keep the money for Isabel and the man she'll fall in love with and marry. I don't have long to live, and a woman doesn't have the right to own property unless she's a widow. You take care of my granddaughter."

Unfortunately, the next day, the posse found the Mallory ranch deserted. The two brothers and Cora Lynn had flown the coop sometime during the night. Deputy McCarthy was called back in town with other issues and he couldn't chase after them, but he placed Damian's picture on a Wanted poster.

CHAPTER 24

Next day at around noon, they were ready to go home. The grandfather took one look at the pink-fringed buggy and declared he was not going to be caught dead in that vehicle. Wayne laughed and offered him his horse to ride. The old man accepted and his dignity preserved, he rode quite well for one so old and pretending to be on the brink of death.

So Wayne drove the buggy with Cousin Celia and John, Renard, Isabel and the old man rode along.

When the ranch house came into view in the distance, John thought he'd never seen a more beautiful sight in his life. This was home. This corner of the world, wild as it still was, with dangers all the time and life often very hard, this was where he belonged.

They stopped in the yard and the ranch hands came to welcome them and to ask a lot of questions. John looked at them smiling and extended his arms to help Isabel from the saddle. Not that she needed any help, but a gentleman was taught this was proper.

"Miss Cecily Richland-Stark, what are you doing here?" cried a shrill voice louder than all the men's voices.

The noise ceased, the good-natured jokes and laughter died and one by one they turned to the front porch where a stern-looking middle-aged woman was surveying the activity in the yard.

To give her her due, Cousin Celia didn't lose her composure. Graciously accepting Wayne's help she climbed down from the buggy seat and twirling her parasol she smiled politely. "On my way going west to San Francisco, I stopped to visit my Cousin John. What about yourself Mrs. Farrell? What are you doing here?"

"Why you, cheeky girl! I came to see what is going on with my wayward son and instead I had to cool my heels for two days because no one was here to talk to. The cook told me that a certain woman called Cousin Celia had lived here with my son, but I never imagined it was you."

"As I said..."

"I know what you said girl and it won't do. There is no cousin Celia that I know of and I should know better. I'm John's mother," the woman cut Celia's word with authority. "But it doesn't matter. He'll do the right thing and marry you."

"Marry?" both Celia and John exclaimed.

"That won't happen, Mrs. Farrell," Celia said.

"Nope," John agreed with her. "The time when you dictated what I have to do is long gone, Mother. I like Cousin Celia very much, but I don't love her and I'm sure she feels the same about me."

"Yes, Mrs. Farrell," Celia nodded.

Renard scratched his red head. "How is she your mother if she's called Mrs. Farrell? Have you been born a bastard, Gorman?"

John's mother glared at him angry, but John explained amused. "Dear Mother kept her maiden name although married legally with my father." No point to wash the family's dirty laundry in public. No point explaining how little consideration and respect his mother had for his father.

"Back to what's important. John, even here in this wild country you should know that you have to marry Cecily. You compromised her in the eyes of the world. And you both should come home to Philadelphia."

Before John could answer, Celia raised her chin and looked at his mother pointedly. "That would be impossible, Mrs. Farrell, unless you want me to be a bigamist. You see I married yesterday morning Wayne Dunbar."

It was John's turn to be surprised. "You married Wayne? But why?"

She turned to Wayne who was waiting near her with a shuttered face. She smiled at him slowly with love in her eyes. "I married him because I love him. Pastor Michelson officiated the ceremony."

"You stupid girl, don't you see that a man like him will rule your life? You won't be able to manipulate him like you did with your father." John's mother bristled at her disappointed that her own plans were ruined.

"Wayne won't rule my life, not in a dictatorial way like you ruled your family. He loves me, you see. He signed a legal paper that my fortune is mine to do what I want with it," Celia said.

"And what are you going to do with it?" Isabel asked curious.

Celia's smile widened. "I'm going to ask my husband what to do. Don't you understand? It's the principle that matters. I'm free to do what I want. And I trust him to give me the best advice."

"Bah," Mrs. Farrell scoffed. "Love doesn't last, if it ever was to start with. What about your life in Philadelphia? What about your family business?"

"I contacted the lawyer and I instructed him to sell everything and transfer all the money to a bank in San Francisco. I'm never returning to Philadelphia." She looked at Wayne again and he squeezed her hand gently in agreement. He'd already told her that as he had no roots anyplace, he was ready to go wherever she wanted.

Understanding that this plan wasn't working, Mrs. Farrell turned to her son. "What about you, John? Are you ready to give up this foolish idea to live here at the end of the world?"

"Maybe you consider this country the end of the world, Mother, but for me this is home. These people are my family. They helped me in difficult times. And I made this ranch a prosperous place," he tried to explain although he knew she won't understand him. She never did.

She zeroed in on Isabel. Sensing her none too friendly scrutiny, Isabel squared her shoulders and straightened her spine.

"This person is your choice?" his mother asked with scorn in her voice.

John stepped near Isabel protectively. "This is Isabel Mallory and she is my guest. She will be treated with courtesy," he said. All of a sudden, he felt tired after everything that happened and he didn't want a confrontation with his mother. Not now, not ever. This was his house and he was the one in charge here, the one making the decisions. His mother had no say in it. "Go home, Mother. There is nothing of interest to you here." Then he turned to his men ignoring her sputtering. "Men, let's celebrate Cousin Celia's wedding and us coming home with good news. I hope Cook has enough food for us."

Isabel led John a merry chase for almost a year before finally agreeing to marry him. And then she surprised John by admitting that she had fallen in love with him from the very first moment she'd seen him, when she still believed he was a gunslinger, living dangerously on the wrong side of the law.

Go figure. John couldn't understand women and their contrary nature. A good thing Isabel accepted to be his wife. He loved her to distraction and he was glad that second guessing her was at an end. Or so he thought.

As for the blond, blue-eyed angel he used to dream of… What angel? All he could think of was a temperamental brunette, with doe-like brown eyes.

She occupied all his dreams.

Celia and Wayne Dunbar traveled west to California and settled north of San Francisco. Celia loved their large house on top of a hill, surrounded by vineyards and Wayne indulged her in every whim she had. He proceeded to build a large shop near the house where he spent most of his time tinkering at his horseless carriage and other mechanical inventions.

Celia's vineyards were very successful producing some of the finest wines in the country. Wayne's inventions not so much, until ten years later when he sold one of his patents to the Ford Motor Company for a lot of money.

Their house was one of the first in the area to have electric lights, running water, and Wayne Dunbar was often seen driving an automobile on the roads of Napa at the amazing speed of ten or even twelve miles per hour.

Celia used to kiss him with love when he was immersed in his work, and then go about running her wine business and taking care of their three children, two girls and a boy. She was one of the first women who shortened her skirts to a more practical length and to cut her hair in a fashionable bob.

They didn't forget their Wyoming cousins and every summer they took their children to Laramie to enjoy riding horses at John Gorman's Diamond G ranch.

So what happened to Toby McDonald and were the Mallorys ever punished for their crimes, you'd ask. The answer is yes, but this is another of the wonderful Tales of Old Wyoming that will be told later.

* * *

Thank you for taking the time to read *Going West.* If you enjoyed it, please consider posting a short review. Word of mouth is the independent author's best friend and much appreciated. Thank you!

Keep reading for an exclusive sneak peek of *Tales Of Old Wyoming* Book 4 – *The Revenge*

The Revenge

VIVIAN SINCLAIR

CHAPTER 1

Laramie, Wyoming Territory, 1888

The house had been abandoned. An eerie silence and a path of destructions welcomed Toby McDonald. Shards of glass from the broken windows covered the floors, furniture pushed around in a fit of rage, paintings thrown to the floors or barely hanging askew on the walls, the elegant Victorian wallpaper with pink roses torn from the walls.

Any man would have been disheartened to see the poor condition of the place and to consider the huge amount of work and money necessary to restore it and bring it to its former glory. Not Toby. This was the grandest house that he'd ever seen. It was even larger than any other rancher's homes where Toby had worked before, not too mention the little cabin where he'd been born. It was a stately two stories with a large wraparound porch.

Yes, it required a lot of work, but Toby was up

to it. Work was all he'd known his entire life. If he closed his eyes he could picture the house in all its splendor, with crystal chandeliers and fine rugs on the gleaming wood floors.

However, for the moment he had to temper down his desire to restore the house. All the money that the lawyer assured him remained in the bank had to be used to buy cattle. His former boss, John Gorman gave him ten heads of cattle to start with, but he needed much more to make the ranch profitable.

There were no cattle on the range and no horses in the barn. It looked like the Mallory brothers had sold everything long before they were forced to run away.

Toby was not worried. It was a good piece of land, a splendid house with a solid barn. It was much more than he'd ever owned and more than he'd ever dreamed to possess. It was something to build on and he had no doubt that with hard work, he'd make it one of the most prosperous places in the area.

Too bad his sister and his little nephew were

not alive to see this dream fulfilled. In their memory he'd work hard and make it.

A loud click of a cocked gun reverberated in the silence of the house and interrupted his dreaming. Shot and left for dead before, Toby was not a man to scare easily. Slowly, he turned to face the gunman.

The newcomer was tall, dark and with his hat pulled low on his brow. His gun was pointed at Toby, but his amused smile showed a perfect row of bright teeth. "Has a tornado destroyed this place?" he asked gesturing with his gun before placing it back in the holster.

"No, just the previous owners wanted to leave me a memory of them," Toby explained wondering if the stranger was friend or foe. "I don't complain though. I'll fix it."

"You bought the ranch from them?"

Toby avoided answering directly. "I'm the new owner, yes. What can I do for you?"

"Nothing, I guess. I had some business in Laramie and I heard they were hiring men good with a gun." He shrugged. "I thought I'll mix my business with earning some money."

"Well, you're a little late. They already killed who they wanted to dispense with, and they ran away as they were wanted by the law," Toby told him hoping this would be the end of it and the stranger would go away. He couldn't stomach more paid killers right now.

The stranger seemed offended. "Wait a minute. I thought they needed protection, not to murder people."

Toby waved his hand tired. "Whatever. They are not here." He couldn't care less of splitting the meaning of the word. A gunfighter was a killer no matter how he chose to interpret it.

The stranger nodded curtly, turned on his heel and left.

Toby looked at the grand piano in the parlor, the only thing that escaped the fury of the Mallorys before leaving. The pleasure of envisioning his future house was gone. The stranger brought with him an air of menace and the reminder that the world was full of dangerous men.

He approached the piano and lifted the lid. His first thought was to get rid of it. What was he to do with a concert piano? Then he changed his mind. Maybe Toby MacDonald had no idea to play the keys, but the instrument was completing the room giving it a special charm. And it kept him motivated to restore the house to the grandeur that it had before the Mallorys destroyed it.

But first he had to see the barn. There were no animals there. He'd have to start there and hire people to work the few cattle he had. Then increase the herd. He went outside. The front door had been torn from its hinges.

He found the stranger sitting on the first step of the porch. "You're still here?"

The stranger stood up and slapped his hat on his leg. "I changed my mind. I think you need me more than the Mallorys did. This place needs a lot of work. You're in luck. I'm here and I'm available."

"I might need," Toby admitted. "But I'll hire ranch hands, not gunfighters."

"I'm good for everything. And by the look of that parlor, those people will not give up easily. They'll be back. For revenge if nothing else. How good are you with a gun?"

Toby shrugged. "As good as I have to be. And you got it wrong. I'm the one who wants revenge, not them. They killed my sister and my nephew."

The stranger whistled. "You definitely need me. I'm staying."

"You don't understand. I could barely afford to pay a ranch help, not a gunfighter," Toby protested exasperated. "Look at this place. Not the house. It's good land, but there are no cattle, no horses, nothing. Whatever little money I have will go toward buying a herd first."

"Good." The stranger placed his hat back on and taking his horse by the bridle went to the barn. Reluctantly Toby followed. How to get rid of a pesky visitor who got in his mind Toby needed him?

Toby tried to think how he felt about the stranger. He was not bad, definitely not. He was not in the same league with the hired gunslingers that killed mindlessly for money. He was so deep in thought, absently following the stranger in the barn that he missed his next words.

"I don't like to be hired and to have a boss. I like to do things my way and to think before I act. Clean," the stranger commented referring to the stall this time. He guided his horse inside and placed a bucket with oats in front of it. Then he turned to Toby smiling. "We can be partners of sorts." Toby opened his mouth to protest, when he raised his hand. "No, I don't want anything in writing. The place is yours. I was referring to the relationship between us only."

Toby blinked. Better if he asked him to leave.

The stranger continued. "As a sign of my good intentions I'll give you some good news. Beyond that outcrop of rocks I saw a bunch of cattle. Not many. About fifty or so. But I think they belong to this ranch and it seems you might need them."

The news was so unexpected and good that Toby felt overwhelmed. Caution thrown aside, he admitted that he needed help and whatever this stranger's hidden plans were, for now it would be easier to accept his help.

"What did you say your name was?" he asked.

"I didn't. The name is Warner. Raymond Warner."

* * *

To find out about new releases and about other books written by Vivian Sinclair visit her website at VivianSinclairBooks.com or follow her on the Author page at Amazon, Facebook at Vivian Sinclair Books, or on GoodReads.com

Tales Of Old Wyoming – western historical fiction

Book 1 – The Younger Brother

Book 2 – A Stranger in Town

Book 3 – Going West

Book 4 – The Revenge

Old West Wyoming Trilogy - western historical fiction

Book 1 - A Western Christmas

Book 2 - The Train To Laramie

Book 3 - The Last Stagecoach

White Christmas Dream – Christmas novels

Book 1 – A Candle In The Window

Book 2 – Christmas At The Ranch

Book 3 – Forgiveness At Christmas

Maitland Legacy, A Family Saga - western contemporary fiction

Book 1 – Lost In Wyoming – Lance's story

Book 2 – Moon Over Laramie – Tristan's story

Book 3 – Christmas In Cheyenne – Raul's

story

Wyoming Christmas Trilogy – western contemporary fiction

Book 1 – Footprints In The Snow – Tom's story

Book 2 – A Visitor For Christmas – Brianna's story

Book 3 – Trapped On The Mountain – Chris' story

Summer Days In Wyoming Trilogy - western contemporary fiction

Book 1 – A Ride In The Afternoon - the Sheriff's story

Book 2 – Fire At Midnight - the Deputy's story

Book 3 – Misty Meadows At Dawn - the Soldier's story

Return To Wyoming - western contemporary fiction

Book 1 - The Christmas Gift

Book 2 - Coming Home For Christmas

Book 3 - Blue Christmas

Book 4 – On A Frosty Christmas Night

Starting Over In Wyoming –western contemporary fiction

Book 1 – Riding Alone

Book 2 – The Old Homestead

Book 3 – On the Hunt

Seattle Rain - women's fiction novels

Book 1 - A Walk In The Rain

Book 2 – Rain, Again!

Book 3 – After The Rain

Virginia Lovers - contemporary romance

Book 1 – Alexandra's Garden

Book 2 – Ariel's Summer Vacation

Book 3 – Lulu's Christmas Wish

A Guest At The Ranch – western contemporary romance

Storm In A Glass Of Water – a small town story